BOUND AND BETRAYED

THE CURSED SOULS SERIES
BOOK TWO

SAMANTHA MORAN

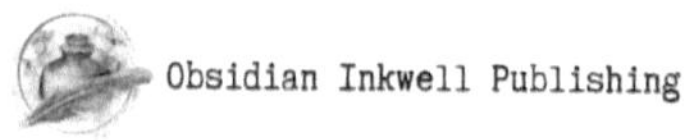 Obsidian Inkwell Publishing

CURSED SOULS SERIES

Dealings in the Dark, 2022
Bound and Betrayed, 2022
Legacy of Lies, Coming Soon

TABLE OF CONTENTS

DEDICATION

This book is dedicated to my two amazing children, Emma and Oliver. You are my everything. Grow up to be healthy, happy, and safe. You are strong and brave and you can be anything that you want to be. Don't ever let anyone tell you that your experiences are invalid. Mommy loves you, always.

AUTHOR'S NOTE

Before reading *Bound and Betrayed,* Cursed Souls Book Two, it would be best to read *Dealings in the Dark,* Cursed Souls Book One.

Bound and Betrayed is a psychological thriller and supernatural horror story that deals with issues related to mental health and possession. As such, the book you are about to read contains adult language, chilling descriptions, graphic scenes depicting physical violence, gore, temporary child death, perceived mental illness, manipulation, isolation, and attempted suicide.

Attitudes held by characters and the actions of characters toward Selena do not reflect the author's beliefs about mental health conditions and those who live with them. These are meant to present social commentary.

If any of these topics are disturbing to you, you may not wish to proceed with this text. Should you decide to continue, thank you for reading *Bound and Betrayed*, the second installment in the Cursed Souls series. I hope you enjoy this spooky tale.

PRAISE FOR DEALINGS IN THE DARK

"I loved this so much! I kept wanting to know what was going to happen next and it kept me at the edge of my seat. Wonderful horror novella!"

-R. Wyer

"This novella kept me up at night wanting to finish it all at once. Easy to read, and easy to "oooh" and "ahhh" at. If you like witchy anything, this is a great, quick read!"

-Marisol C.

"This was a riveting, fast-paced story. Ms. Moran's ability to paint a dark, hellish picture has few equals, if any. When all is said and done, you will absolutely need to pick up book two, Bound and Betrayed."

-Brian S.

"If you like all things spooky, supernatural, and witchy,

this is the book to read! [...] I cannot wait for book #2! I need to know more about that ending!"

    -Sarah B.

"When I heard the premise for *Dealings in the Dark* and saw the cover, I ran to find my Kindle! This was the perfect spooky season read to get me out of my slump [...] With the way this book ended, I cannot wait to read book two! The twist at the end of this was just phenomenal."

    -Kassie G.

"...This novella had so many great moments that put you on the edge of your seat. This is a must read!"

    -Marissa C.

"This novella is a fun, spooky read, perfect for a quiet and chilly autumn evening. It's got all sorts of goodies for lovers of the supernatural: a delightfully naughty demon of the crossroads, a practicing witch who happens to be desperate, a binding contract, running water, bad decisions, an unexpected conclusion (which I did NOT see coming and thoroughly enjoyed), and a VERY bad dog. [...] Give this one a read."

    -Paul M.

*Excerpts from these reviews have been included with the reviewers' express permissions.

DEALINGS IN THE DARK: SUMMARY

In *Dealings in the Dark*: Cursed Souls Book One, Alexandria Hendricks, a twenty-seven year old witch, found herself in a predicament she did not know how to handle.

When her grandmother, Elizabeth Hendricks, moved to an assisted living facility due to a decline in her mental health, Alexandria had to learn how to handle her ancestral magick on her own for the first time. But, a demon sensed her newfound weakness and took advantage of her vulnerability.

Sending a hellhound to stalk Alexandria, Iroth orchestrated a scenario in which she was forced to summon him to her plane in exchange for a favor. Instead of calling off the hound, Iroth called in an eighteen-year-old debt, a contract nine-year-old Alexandria foolishly signed in exchange for saving her best friend's life. He tasked her with finding and returning his silver ring, a powerful occult object that both contained the essence of the demon and maintained his immortality. Should she fail, he promised to murder her and claim her soul for eternity in two days' time.

Reluctantly, Alexandria agreed to perform his task. The

challenge of finding Iroth's missing ring forced her to dig deep into family secrets and disturbing knowledge her grandmother had long kept from her. Through her grandmother's journals, Alexandria learned that she had died as a child and been revived through yet another illicit deal with a demon that her mother, Corinne, made many years before. In return, her grandmother sought revenge against the demon Iroth for Corinne's horrific death, binding her own essence to the ring in order to weaken Iroth and drain him of his immortality.

After harrowing escapes from Iroth's hellhound, CeCe, Alexandria managed to use Iroth's own essence against him, defeating him in a show of strength and wit. But, in the end, it cost her more than she bargained for when Iroth's master, a demon masquerading as her childhood friend Selena, claimed her essence as a replacement for the demon she lost.

BOUND AND BETRAYED

THEY SAID IT WAS ALL IN MY HEAD,
THAT DEMONS WEREN'T REAL.
THEY WERE WRONG.

MONDAY, OCTOBER 4TH

CHAPTER ONE

MONDAY AFTERNOON

"S\u1d07\u029f\u1d07\u0274\u1d00?"

Dr. Holland's voice draws me back to reality. Without even knowing, I had been lost in thought.

How long have I been dissociating?

"Hmm? Sorry..."

"You were far away for a little while. Where did you go?"

"I..." I begin, but the words die on my tongue.

Dr. Holland waits patiently as I stare at the tip of my shoe and draw circles on her otherwise perfect shag rug. I know she's watching me. She's always watching and waiting during our sessions.

"I'm sorry," I continue. "I'm tired."

"Have you been sleeping well? Still having nightmares?"

I nod. I've been having nightmares for eighteen years. It seems unlikely to change anytime soon.

"Do you want to talk about them?" Her voice is calm and gentle, as always.

For the last five years, Dr. Holland has been my psychiatrist. She's the most recent in a long line of counselors, therapists, psychologists, and psychiatrists, each possessing or preferring a different title. She's the best one I've had so far.

It took them eight years to let me out of my in-patient treatment. When I became an adult and demonstrated no plans or desire to harm myself or others, the treatment center had no legal reason to hold me any longer.

There were so many different doctors and nurses in the facility that I've lost count. None of them listened, though. None of them helped.

When I was released, my parents found Dr. Llovero. I didn't like him at all. He was pushy, always asking the wrong questions. He treated me like a child. I stopped seeing him after nearly a year. My parents were profoundly disappointed.

The next one was Dr. Branson. She was okay. I found her online. I didn't have to leave my room for our appointments. I liked that. It felt safer. She and I made progress for a time, but then she got married and had to leave the practice because she moved out of state. That was difficult. I don't like being left behind.

Dr. Holland came after her. I like Dr. Holland well enough. She listens to me, like actually listens. She doesn't interrupt and ask stupid questions. She waits and watches. Sometimes she watches for a very long time without saying a word. It was uncomfortable at first, but I've gotten used to it now. I have to come to her office for our visits, but she has a nice, welcoming space.

The couches here are soft, not like the leather ones that Dr. Llovero had in his office. They don't creak when I move or stick to my legs when I wear shorts. There are plenty of blankets and pillows around in case I get cold or want to hide behind them.

One of the pillows is a very bright blue and shaped like a heart. That's my favorite.

I like the art on the walls, too. There are lots of drawings from her younger patients and some cool paintings and photographs from her older ones. She even hung one of mine.

Last year, I took a picture of an old treehouse in the woods. I don't know how I found it. It felt like I had been there a thousand times before. My feet simply carried me back and back, past the running creek and a freaky old abandoned building.

The treehouse looked like the usual kind of place where kids used to play. The walls were painted sloppily. There were crayon drawings near the bottom. There was even a raggedy old curtain that served as a door. It waved to me in the wind. I think that's why I climbed up. It was almost like being invited. I know that seems silly, but it's true.

The idea of the treehouse was striking, I guess. I could picture a small group of kids up there playing during the long, hot, summer days. But, it hadn't been taken care of in a while. Something about the way it looked, the emptiness of it, resonated with me. So, I crouched in the doorway under the shredded fabric and snapped the picture.

I printed one copy and hung it up on my wall. I stared at that picture for a month before I brought Dr. Holland a copy, too. She politely thanked me and set it up in a nice bronze frame, then hung it up by the window directly across from the couch.

I keep waiting for her to ask me about the picture, but she hasn't yet. I stare at it for a while and wonder why that stupid picture matters so much. I don't know yet. I'll figure it out eventually.

Dr. Holland says that we figure most things out eventually. Maybe she'll figure me out. I hope so.

"Selena?" she prompts me again.

"Yeah, sorry. I'm... Sorry. I guess I don't really remember much about what happened in the dream last night. I just remember how it made me feel."

"That happens to me after nightmares, too. Feelings tend to linger longer than the events themselves. Can you tell me about how you felt?"

I reach for the heart-shaped pillow and hold it on my lap, leaning back against the couch. The little pillow has a patch of sequins that change colors when you flip them. I drag my fingers through them, watching the colors change.

"I was afraid."

"Okay. Do you remember why?"

I squeeze my eyes shut and concentrate, trying to drift back into the memory of the dream. "I remember... running. I was running from something."

"What were you running from?"

I try to picture it, but whatever it was won't come into focus. "I don't remember. I'm sorry."

"Don't push yourself too hard. Let your mind still. If you're meant to remember, it will come to you."

'Let my mind still.' She uses that phrase a lot. I try. I do. But, it doesn't always work. Maybe I'm doing something wrong? That doesn't surprise me at all. I never seem to do the right thing.

"Practice your breath work," she reminds me. "Breathe in, hold, and release."

I do. It helps a little.

"I don't think it was a person."

"Good. What do you think it was?"

"I don't know. An animal? A dog, maybe?"

"You dream of dogs often. Would it surprise you if you were having a nightmare about a dog?"

"No."

I do dream of dogs a lot. Not the soft, lovable kind. I like those well enough. My parents used to have one when I was growing up. They even brought him to visit me at the facility a couple of times. His name was Max. I thought it was kind of a stupid name. We played in the courtyard and I scratched him behind the ears. He was funny. He kicked the ground so hard when he got scratches. I liked him.

No, my nightmares aren't filled with dogs like Max. They're filled with the kind of dogs that have horrifying rows of razor-sharp teeth, lines and lines of them like sharks.

Dr. Holland says that the freaky dogs from my dreams aren't real. She says they're just a manifestation of childhood fears. I want to believe her. Max didn't have teeth like that, and I don't think I've ever met a dog that did. But, I don't know. I have no idea why I dream of terrifying dogs. There's so much that I can't remember. I wish I could tell what's real and what's not. My life would be so much easier if I could trust my own mind.

I've never known what that feels like. So many people have told me that the things I see and hear, the things that feel so real, are figments of my imagination. They have to be right. It's me against all of them. They have the numbers. I'm all alone.

I rein myself in. A pity party won't solve anything. I've wasted too much time lost in my thoughts during this session already.

"I remember that it was late at night. And, it was so cold. The kind of cold that lets you see your breath. I was breathing so hard. The little clouds kept getting in the way. I had to keep swatting at them, but the more I swatted, the thicker they got."

"In your dream or when you were awake?" she asks.

"In my dream."

She scribbles something on her paper, then looks up and gives me a reassuring smile.

"And there was this strange laughter. Someone was laughing at me."

"Laughing?" she asks, shifting in her chair and taking notes.

"Yeah, laughing. It wasn't scary by itself, the laughing. But, with the dog... Well, I think it was a dog. I don't know. It sounded cruel, I guess? Like, the woman was happy that I was so scared..."

"Did you recognize the woman's voice? Was it someone you knew?"

"Sort of," I answer. "It was very familiar, but I can't quite place the voice. I don't know if it belongs to a real person or not."

"Mmm." She scribbles something else down, then sits the pad of paper on her lap.

"I don't think I remember anything else."

"That's fine. You've done well today, Selena. I know it's hard to talk about your dreams. Thank you for sharing this with me."

I nod. She's right. It is hard to talk about stuff like this. People already think I'm crazy. I see things that they don't see, and I hear things that others don't. Well, I used to anyway. Now I take about six different medications to keep the hallucinations at bay. But, people around town know. If I say the wrong thing... I trust Dr. Holland well enough, but word gets around. I've learned that the walls can have ears. I'm tired of the stares and the whispers. More importantly, I don't want to get sent back to the treatment center.

The treatment center was awful. I'll take the nightmares and whispers from the shadows over a stay at the facility any day.

Dr. Holland glances down at her watch. "We've run out of time today. Do you feel like you need another session tomorrow to talk about this dream, or should we keep with our regular Thursday appointment?"

"Thursday will be fine."

"I'm going to think about this dream. I want to look over some of our past sessions to see if I can help you draw any connections to things we've discussed before. Would it be alright if we spoke more about it on Thursday, then?"

"Sure," I answer. I set the pillow aside and begin to stand.

"Selena?" Dr. Holland interjects.

I stop and look up. Her usual kind smile is plastered on her face. I used to think it was fake. I'm not sure anymore. She seems nice. Things aren't always what they seem, though.

"Have you been drinking your water and taking your medications like we talked about?"

I blush. I knew she wouldn't let me get away without it.

"I try. I don't like the way some of the pills make me feel."

"I understand," she says. She clicks her shiny black pen, sending the tip back inside. "I want you to try though, especially with your new medication. It will take some time to adjust. If it isn't taken properly, it won't work as it should. Can you try again?"

"I will." I turn to walk toward the office door.

"While we are on the topic of medications, let's try to take some time off from the sleeping pills this week. Just for a few days, okay?"

"Why?" I ask. "I need them." My hand is on the doorknob, but I don't turn it.

"Sometimes, they can make dreams more intense. If the nightmares are bothering you more lately, it might be helpful to take a short break. Just for a few days."

That makes sense, I guess. I could use a break from the vivid dreams. The problem is, I can't sleep without the pills. I take them every night. I have since I was ten. Without them, I doubt I'll even be able to sleep at all.

I don't want to argue about them with Dr. Holland. If I do, she might stop prescribing them altogether. I can't have that. So instead, I just say, "Okay."

"Okay." Dr. Holland stands and moves behind her desk.

She unlocks the drawer and drops the notepad inside, then retrieves another, probably for her next patient. She always takes her notes on paper. I like that. I don't know why.

"Don't forget to do your journal work," she prompts as I step into the hall. "I'll see you on Thursday!"

I pull the office door closed behind me and pass through the small waiting room, making my way to the exit. An older, balding man smiles at me as I pass. I see him here often. He seems nice enough, I guess. We don't talk though. Patients aren't supposed to talk to each other. Not that I would want to, anyway...

Before I make it outside, Dr. Holland greets him warmly.

"Stanley, it's good to see you. Come on in."

I see him stand and collect his things, then disappear into Dr. Holland's office. She flashes one more reassuring smile at me before she closes the door behind her.

I check my phone. The bus will be here in about ten minutes. Out of habit, I dig my earbuds out of my pocket and stick them in. I use these every day, too. The world can be too much sometimes. Too many voices. Too many sudden noises. Too many people watching me.

I open up my music on my phone and it immediately starts playing. The heavy beat drowns out the noise of the passing train. I stuff my hands into my pockets and check for traffic. Breathing in the humid early autumn air, I head off in the direction of the bus stop.

OCTOBER 4TH

Mom and dad are leaving for Colorado in the morning. They'll be gone until Sunday for Andrea's wedding. I'll have to fend for myself for the next few days.

I can do this. I think...

At least I have leftover lasagna. Mom's lasagna has always been my favorite food. She makes everything from scratch. It's gooey and hot, and all-around delicious. She grows her own tomatoes and fresh garlic out back to make huge pots of sauce every summer. She uses the fresh herbs she grows on the kitchen windowsill, too. Her grandmother taught her how to do that when she was little, and she's tried to teach me, but I've never been very good at it. I burnt the sauce once. She stopped asking me to help after that.

Tonight though, I know that she only made it because she feels guilty that she and dad are leaving for their trip in the morning. There are enough leftovers to feed a family of ten, even though it's just the three of us.

It's always been just the three of us. That's my fault. They wanted to have another kid before I ended up in the treatment center. They stopped trying after that. I can't blame them, I suppose. Who would want another kid when their first kid turned out like me?

I'm twenty-eight years old, and they're still afraid to leave me home alone for more than twenty-four hours. I still require supervision. It makes me feel like a burden.

I am a burden.

Mom will never admit that, though. She's the most selfless person I know. That makes it even worse. I wish I could be a normal adult and move out, give her back her own life. But, I need my parents. I can't live alone.

I'll just have to be extra convincing tomorrow so that she doesn't cancel their trip. They deserve a break from constantly monitoring me.

Dr. Holland suggested that I should stop taking my sleeping pills for a little while because of how bad the nightmares have been. She says that the pills can make the dreams worse. I don't know if it's better to take the pills and sleep, even if I still have nightmares, or to not take the pills and stay awake all night. I know that's what's going to happen. I can't sleep without them.

I shouldn't be afraid of the dark. That's what everyone says, anyway. They tell me I don't have to be afraid of the shadows anymore. I want to believe them. I'm trying to believe them. It's just... sometimes the shadows whisper to me.

I will try not to take them tonight. I hope she's right.

TUESDAY, OCTOBER 5TH

CHAPTER TWO

EARLY TUESDAY MORNING

IT'S WELL AFTER MIDNIGHT, BUT WITHOUT MY PILLS, I'M FAR TOO wired to sleep. There's too much tension in my muscles, and even with Dr. Holland's breathwork strategy, I can't force myself to feel still. Nothing works. All I can do is hunker down in my bed beneath my thick comforter and wait for morning to come.

In the living room, my grandma's old clock ticks loudly through the night. The constant ticking sets my teeth on edge. To make matters worse, it marks the hours with a heavy chime, each one leaving me feeling more foolish than the last. It's dumb, but the chimes seem like they're mocking me, judging me for my paranoia.

I squeeze my eyes tightly shut. *I'm an adult. Adults shouldn't be afraid of the dark. This is ridiculous.*

Anxious thoughts race through my mind. My heart beats rapidly inside my chest, bouncing around between my ribs like a rubber ball. I try to distract myself by listening to its steady rhythm, but the distraction doesn't last long. The disturbing sounds of the night keep ripping me away from what little comfort I manage to find.

My parents' house is old. During the day, the house is beautiful. It's not huge, but it's big enough for us. I have the loft and bathroom upstairs, and mom and dad have the master and bathroom below. But, when the weather turns cold, it creaks and groans, settling on its foundation. It makes the house feel as though it's alive, a monster we have naively chosen to inhabit as it waits to devour us whole.

Despite my countless sessions with Dr. Holland, my imagination runs wild. Everything is always so much worse at night.

My eyes pop open of their own accord. I toss and turn, hearing every noise and seeing every shifting shadow. I stare so long at the inky darkness in the corner by my closet that it appears to swirl unnaturally. Unwittingly, I conjure up images of smoky figures with long, talon-like fingers waiting for me to fall asleep before they attack. I grimace at the thought of those spindly hands grabbing at my ankles or digging into my flesh. My paranoia increases to the point that I can even faintly smell something disgusting coming from within the shadows.

What is it? Smoke? Rotten eggs? Where could that smell be coming from?

My imagination. That's where it's coming from. Dr. Holland keeps telling me that I have a highly creative mind that chooses to manifest its abilities in disturbing ways because of my childhood trauma. She says it's a way of processing the truth of what happened in that basement. It's just... if what I remember isn't real, I have no idea what that truth might be. I have no clue what happened down there. And if I don't know, neither does she. So, how can she be so sure?

I hate that I can't help but doubt everything. It's exhausting.

What I remember can't be real. The memories feel so real, but everyone says that I'm wrong. Every single doctor I've ever seen. *They have to be right though, don't they?* So many of them have come to the same conclusion.

No, the memories can't be real. There's something wrong with me. A lot of things, really. I mean, who would make up something as horrific as that? Only someone who's truly messed up.

I wish I could remember what my mind has been hiding from me for all these years. If I could figure that out, maybe this constant fear would ebb away.

I'm so tired of being afraid.

A heavy wind blows through the red maple outside of my window, and the branches sway violently, tapping against the panes of glass. The tips screech ominously as they pull away. The sound makes me shiver. Goosebumps erupt across my skin.

The pale light of the moon filters through the tree's vibrant leaves, setting the branches ablaze with imaginary fire. Hidden within the leaves, glowing red eyes watch me. They blink in and out of existence as the wind rises again.

I pull my comforter up to my chin and cower.

In the dark, I'm a small child again, wanting desperately to climb out of bed and race over to my dresser where my lamp sits. I want to fill the whole space with the safety of light. But, I don't. I can't. My parents have always been light sleepers, and their room is directly below my own. I don't want to worry them. They'll hear my footsteps and they'll come up here to check on me. If they see me sleeping with the light on again, they'll call Dr. Holland, and I'll have to go back for another session tomorrow. They'll probably even cancel their trip. I can't let them do that. I can't disappoint them.

So, I do my best to convince myself that Dr. Holland is right.

My mind is seeing things that aren't there. I am in my room, safe and alone. There are no monsters in the shadows waiting to devour me. There are no glowing eyes in the trees. I'm being unreasonable. I need to still myself. I need to rein in my imagination.

I squeeze my eyes shut again and take three shaky breaths. I draw the air in, hold it, and release, focusing on the way it makes me feel, trying to calm my frenzied pulse. I repeat Dr. Holland's mantra:

"I am safe. I am in control. I am going to be alright."

That's when the voices begin.

They're subtle at first, whispers easily mistaken for the rustling of the maple's leaves. I only recognize them because I've heard them so many times before. Many of them layer over each other. They're dry and scratchy, deep.

I try to ignore them. They don't like that at all.

The voices grow louder, more insistent, as I roll over and face away from the window. My name is called out over and over again until it nearly loses its meaning. The voices jumble together, an absolute cacophony: "Selena, Selena, Selena."

"Leave me alone," I whisper. "You're not real. Leave me alone."

They'll never leave me alone.

The laughter from my nightmares breaks through the din, rising above the grating voices of the others. It echoes around the room, enveloping me. Her laughter is soft and gentle, like a mother watching a young child do something silly. It's such a stark contrast to the voices of the others. Somehow, that makes it so much worse. It suffocates me. I don't understand why something so seemingly sweet can send such a strong, revolting chill down my spine.

The worst part is that even if they tried, no one else could hear her. They never do. This torture is for me alone.

"Selena," she croons. "It's almost time, darling. It's almost time."

I struggle to catch my breath as the panic sets in. Hot tears roll down my face and drip onto my pillow.

"Go away. Go away. Go away!"

My last rejection comes out louder than I intend. I'll be lucky if my parents don't hear it. Guilt mingles with my terror as I bury my face in the pillow, muffling the sound of my fearful sobs.

It's not real. It's not real. It's not real.

"Soon," the soft female voice continues. "We will be together again, you and I. Oh, how I've missed you. Don't resist me, darling. It will only make it worse. Or do, I suppose." She chuckles again. "It won't matter. You will always let me in. You have no choice. Very, very soon..."

I pull the pillow tight against my face and cram the fluffy padding over my ears. I desperately want to drown her out.

It makes no difference. My ears were never the problem. Her voice is inside my head.

The problem is me.

I wish it would stop. *Please, make it stop. Please, make it stop. Make it stop. Make it stop. Make it stop!*

But it doesn't stop. Not until the sun finally rises.

I grow increasingly numb as the hours wear on. Everything I am is drained. I'm a dead battery. I'm a hollowed-out tree.

Red-eyed and exhausted, I'm still awake when my mother pulls back the living room curtains in the morning.

CHAPTER THREE

LATER TUESDAY MORNING

"Are you sure you'll be okay?" Mom asks.

"I'll be fine. I promise."

Dad loads up the last suitcase and gives me a reassuring smile, followed by a little shoulder squeeze. He never says much, but he doesn't have to. He worries too, just not as much as her. She worries enough for all three of us.

"She'll be fine, Judy." He cocks his head to the side and gestures for Mom to get in the car, but she hesitates. "If we don't get on the road, we're going to miss our flight."

She starts to turn away then stops, eyeing me warily. "It's just... we've never been gone for so long before."

She's trying to be subtle, but her words aren't hard to translate: "We've never left you alone for so long because we're worried about what you'll do if we're not around."

I stare down at the gravel driveway and softly toe aside a small red rock. I don't know what to say to make her feel better. I'm worried, too. I can't let her know that, though.

For once, I want to be mature. I want to let them have their fun. They'll only be gone for five days. They haven't had a vacation in years, and every other time they've gone somewhere, they've been forced to drag me along with them. That's not a break. Not really. Besides, they haven't seen Andrea since she was twelve. They deserve this, and I'm doing my best to give it to them, to take care of them for once.

I borrow from my positive self-speak training to strengthen my resolve. I should be able to handle five days. It's not like I'm in the middle of nowhere. There's a bus stop up the road by the creek, and our town may be small, but it has all the basics: food, coffee, pharmacy, and even an urgent care. I know how to take care of myself. I have to do it alone for a short time, that's all.

It will only be five days. What's the worst that can happen?

Thoughts of my ten-year-old self bleeding out in Alexandria's basement surge to the surface, but I shove them down. *That won't happen again. It never happened in the first place. Everything will be fine.*

I clear my throat and offer her small reassurances. "You left me enough lasagna to feed a small army. I promise to eat. And, I'll go to work and therapy, and I'll drink water and take my meds. I can even call and check in if you want. You don't have to worry."

She glances over at Dad. He nods.

"Selena is an adult. She knows what to do."

"Okay," she replies. It's obvious that she's trying to convince herself that he's right. "Okay. Good. Well, I left the number for the hotel on the fridge. Oh, and Stacy's boy Stephen is home from school this semester. She said something about academic probation. I don't know. But, he's just down the road if something happens."

"Stephen. Got it."

"And I left a little extra money in the bread box, just in case."

"Okay."

"Judy..." Dad urges. "It's time to go."

Mom wraps me in a tight embrace. It feels like she'll never let me go. I hug her back and let her kiss my cheek before she finally releases me and backs away.

"I love you, baby."

"I love you, too. Have a nice trip."

"Be careful."

"I will."

Dad opens her car door and helps her inside. They've been married for thirty-three years and he still opens every door for her. That makes me smile.

As he rounds the rear of the car, he stops. "Take your medicine, Selena. Promise me?"

Shame creeps into my cheeks. I hate that they doubt me so much. He means well, though.

"I promise."

"Love you, kid."

"Love you, too. Get her a drink at the airport. She needs it."

"10/4."

He pulls open his own door and slips inside without looking back, honking the horn as they drive away. Mom waves somberly in the mirror. I wave back.

She thinks I'll lose my mind before they come back home.

Their car turns out of the driveway, leaving behind a trail of dust. Suddenly, I find myself alone.

My grandma's antique clock, one of mom's most prized possessions, chimes as I softly close the door behind me. The reverberation of the bells echoes off the walls. It's nine o'clock. I have nowhere to be until noon.

I look around the empty house before me. Everything is calm and still. It's so quiet. Something about the reality that I will be the only living creature in my home for the next five days makes it feel cold. I've been alone for several hours before, but never for an extended period of time like this. It's unnerving.

My footsteps echo on the hardwood as I cross the living room and pick up the remote, turning on the tv to fill the void. Dad's morning news program appears on the screen. A woman stands in front of a weather map, gesturing at little swirls of wind heading our way.

"Unseasonable temperatures will create a bit of a mess for local weather over the next several days. Expect significant drops, especially in the mornings, followed by periods of unanticipated heat and humidity. Residents should..."

With the silence broken, I head off to the kitchen for breakfast. Briefly, I consider reheating mom's lasagna, but as I rifle through the contents of the fridge, I discover a little carton of the farm-fresh eggs I love from the stand down the street. Mom must have restocked these before she left. The small gesture makes me smile.

I take these out instead, inspecting the variety of colors. Selecting one brown egg and one green, I retrieve a small pan from the neatly hung rack above the island. Humming quietly to myself, I crack the eggs into a bowl and add a dash of milk, then pour them into the hot pan and scramble them up. They're nothing like the fluffy eggs mom usually makes, but they smell delicious and make my mouth water, anyway. I add seasonings and push them around until they're solid. Then, I turn off the heat and let them sit in the hot pan to finish.

I'm hungrier than I have any right to be after eating so much last night, so I grab an everything bagel out of the pantry and drop it into the toaster, pushing the button for "bagel" and turning the knob to "3". Impatiently, I lean forward onto my elbows and tap my fingers on the counter, but before the bagel even pops up, the droning of the news program disappears, plunging the house back into heavy silence.

The power is out.

"Great," I mumble. I roll my eyes and push myself away from the counter, making my way into my parents' bedroom.

Little clouds of dust fly through the air as I lift the large framed picture of my parents on their honeymoon, revealing the electrical panel hidden behind it. Judging by the amount of build-up, we haven't lost power in a while. I swat the air and cough, then lay the frame gently on the bed.

I tug on the latch of the gray panel door. It pops open easily enough, revealing a series of carefully labeled black switches. Every breaker is off. That strikes me as odd. We must have had a serious power surge for all of them to go down at once, but I don't know why that would have happened. I've seen the vacuum shut a room or two off at a time, but I haven't heard of the whole house going down at once. And, as far as I know, there weren't any power-sucking appliances running. I highly doubt the toaster would cause this.

With a shrug and a series of heavy clicks, I flip each breaker back on, one by one: master, living room, kitchen, dining room, loft.

The faint hum of electricity whirs as lights and fans come to life throughout the house. Then, all at once, every noise-making doodad stirs to life.

Next to the bed, Dad's alarm clock buzzes and flashes

angrily. I shut the thing off, punching in the correct time. In the living room, the sports segment drones on, ranting about the lack of defense in the last game. Somehow, even though no one has touched the remote, the volume is twice as loud as it was before. At the same time, the kitchen stereo blasts country music and the microwave clock incessantly beeps.

The chaos of it all makes me cringe. Suddenly, the heavy silence from before doesn't seem so bad after all.

I pull out my phone and use the app to turn off all of the lights before closing the door and re-hanging the picture over the panel, making a mental note to reset all of the other clocks before leaving for work. Systematically weaving my way through each room, I turn down the volume on the tv, shut off the stereo, and silence the microwave. By the time everything is set, my eggs are ice cold.

"Awesome."

I pop my eggs onto a plate and stick them in the microwave for 30 seconds. While they're heating up again, I finally manage to toast my bagel. I schmear it with cream cheese and sprinkle on some everything seasoning, then dump my now rubbery eggs on top.

Just as I take a bite of my less-than-satisfying breakfast, the power goes out again.

"Ugh!" I complain. Annoyed, I leave my plate on the counter and march back into my parents' room. I drop the picture on the bed again and open the panel door.

This time, all the switches are on.

"What?"

Confused, I cross their room to the windows and pull back one of the curtains. Though last night had been windy and the meteorologist predicted more wind to come, the trees are absolutely still. There shouldn't be anything wrong with the power lines, and this time I know nothing was going on in the house that would cause a problem like this...

I drop the curtain back into place, shaking my head.

That's when I hear the creaking sounds of footsteps on the old wooden floor upstairs.

I freeze. My parents are gone. I watched them drive away. We don't have any pets. There's no one here but me.

So, why is there someone in my room?

As suddenly as they started, the footsteps stop.

My ears strain as I continue to listen with bated breath, eyes wide in fear.

After a few moments, they begin again.

The creaking sounds cross the room repeatedly as though someone is pacing from my window to the loft railing and back, over and over again. This continues for several minutes.

They stop once more.

Very slowly, I crouch down and reach beneath my parents' bed for their heavy wooden baseball bat. Mom always keeps it on hand for nightly home defense. Right now, I'm thankful that I'm not the only family member in this house with some form of paranoia.

As quietly as I can, I tiptoe through the room to their door and scan the first floor. I can't see anyone from here. The dining room is around the corner, out of my line of sight. There could be someone in there. My loft is above me. I can't see up there, either.

Nervous sweat beads on my brow as I take one small step into the living room and press my back against the wall. I clutch the bat close to my chest and steady my shaky breathing, inching my way toward the stairs. A part of me foolishly wants to call out, "Hello! Who's there?" I squash it down. I may be a lot of things, but stupid isn't one of them. I know better than to announce my presence to intruders like that.

With each step toward the stairs, more and more of the dining room comes into view. The space is empty. I let out a small breath of relief. That means that whoever is in my room is alone. At least I'm not outnumbered.

I have to go upstairs.

I don't want to go upstairs.

I tremble as I reach the railing and cast my eyes up. I can't see anyone from here, so with nimble feet, I tiptoe to the other side of the staircase and press myself against that wall, trying to stay out of sight.

I count the stairs to the loft. *Thirteen. Only thirteen stairs separate me from the invader that has found their way into my home.*

Trembling, I begin my ascent.

Halfway up the stairs, the creaking of footsteps begins again, forcing me to a halt. They're by the closet, but if the pattern holds, they'll be back over this way soon. When they come this way, they'll be able to see me. I only have two options: run away or surprise them.

I've made up my mind before I even realize it. Gripping the bat's handle tightly, I charge up the stairs.

At the top, I skid to a stop. There's no one here.

"That's not possible."

Someone was in my room. Someone was pacing back and forth. There has to be someone up here.

My bathroom door is wide open, exactly as I left it this morning. There's nowhere for anyone to hide in the small space, even if they tried.

Where are they?

A realization strikes me as I stare at my closet.

Bat raised high above my head, I approach the slightly cracked door. With a final deep breath, I slam it open with my foot.

Only clothes and years of piled-up junk occupy the space. I am alone.

"That's not possible," I say again, incredulously. "That's not possible."

But, it's the truth. I am alone.

Shaking, I stumble back to my bed and sit. I drop the heavy bat to the floor with an echoing thud and hold my head in my hands.

I had been so sure. The sounds were so real. *But, they're always so real, aren't they? Why had I let myself believe this time would be any different? It's not usually footsteps, but I hear things that aren't there all the time...*

Stupid. I am being stupid. I'm better than this. I let my fear and paranoia get the best of me again. I can't let that happen this week. I have to be an adult. I have to know the difference between what's real and what's in my head.

I sigh, embarrassed and disappointed in myself. *It hasn't even been an hour.*

How am I supposed to survive alone?

I jump half out of my skin as the power returns, resurrecting the chaos below. Rolling my eyes, I flop back on my bed and stare up at the slanted ceiling.

"Good morning, Selena. Get your shit together."

OCTOBER 5TH

I didn't sleep at all last night. I was right about not taking the pills. I really hoped I wouldn't be, but I was. Anyway, I'm exhausted today.

Mom and Dad left for their trip a couple of hours ago. Things are already not going well. As soon as they left, the power went out -

TWICE. That, along with no sleep, must have been fuel for my over-active imagination. I could have sworn I heard footsteps in my room. I checked the whole house, though. There's no one here but me.

It's not the first time I've heard things that aren't there. I should have known better. When will I learn? Dr. Holland and my parents keep telling me that I'm safe in this house. <u>I AM safe in this house</u>. The only one putting me in danger is myself. If I would just chill out, everything would be fine.

Why can't I be like other people? I want to be like them so badly.

I've got work in about an hour, so I'm going to do the whole self-care thing Mom is always going on about. Shower, shave, teeth, deodorant, deep breathing.

I wish I could drive. I get why they won't let me have a license, but I hate having to catch the bus all the time.

Anyway, this day has to get better. I'm going to manifest that, or whatever. At least I'll be busy at work. Busy is good.

CHAPTER FOUR

TUESDAY AFTERNOON

A SENSE OF UNEASE LINGERS FOR A LONG TIME AFTER THE POWER comes back on. I should feel relieved after searching the entire house and finding nothing, yet even though I am fully aware that I'm being ridiculous, I can't help but feel like I'm being watched.

There was no fiendish creature lurking in the depths of my closet. No axe murderer was hiding underneath my bed.

Still, every once in a while a ripple of goosebumps washes over me. I swear that no matter where I go, I can sense a heavy presence behind me and an odd pressure on the back of my head. I keep seeing things move out of the corner of my eye. I'm rubbing my arms raw, trying to force the tiny hairs to lay flat. It doesn't work.

I'm nearly certain that all of this is in my head. Nearly...

I can't help but feel like prey, like a deer watched by a hungry wolf hidden beyond the edge of the trees.

I try to force down my cold bagel sandwich, but after the

massive surge of adrenaline, I'm far too nauseated to eat. The tiny framed picture of my mom watches me judgmentally as I drop the remnants of my breakfast into the trash.

"Yeah, yeah. I know. Sorry..."

I promise myself that I'll eat later.

Before getting ready for my shift at the library, I reluctantly climb the stairs to my bedroom and take out my leather-bound journal. It was a birthday gift from Dr. Holland. She insists that writing down my experiences and feelings will help me work out some of my fear and confusion. Sometimes it does, and sometimes it doesn't. I use it anyway. It would be rude not to.

My hands have finally stopped shaking, so I scribble a quick entry about my "auditory hallucination." That's what she calls the stuff I hear that no one else does. This time, writing about it helps a little. I'm glad.

I still have an hour before my shift, so I decide to take a very long, very hot shower. My neck and shoulder muscles are so tight that it hurts to turn my head. It's probably from tossing and turning all night. I should have taken the sleeping pills. Now, all of my muscles are bunched up in knots. Of course, I'm sure chasing an imaginary invader through the house with a heavy baseball bat didn't help with that, either.

I keep making mistakes. When am I going to learn?

A wall of steam greets me when I step out of the shower into my tiny bathroom. I dry myself as quickly as I can and stare at my reflection in the mirror. There are deep, dark circles beneath my eyes.

I can't go to work looking like this. My manager will send me straight home.

With a sigh, I brush my pale blonde hair and braid it while it's still wet. It won't dry in time for my shift anyway, and I can't handle the extra effort it would take to pull out the hair dryer and struggle with it right now. Quickly, I brush my teeth and smear a little concealer under my eyes. It doesn't fix the problem, but it does take the edge off. To distract from the shadows that remain, I add a little mascara.

I kind of look like a functional human being. Good enough.

The air outside the bathroom is freezing when I step out and slip into my work clothes. Thank goodness for the fuzzy black pullover we had to buy when the Teen Reading Room was remodeled last year. It's warm, and I hug my arms close to me, savoring the comfortable feeling.

When I'm finally ready to leave, I triple-check the locks on the door and pop my headphones into my ears. The deep bass of one of my favorite albums drowns out the noise of the world around me. This morning has been stressful enough. The last thing I need is to start jumping at every little sound.

Living with constant paranoia is difficult. Of course, it's made worse when my mind creates things that aren't there just to torture me. The music helps. It keeps the whispers away.

It doesn't take me long to walk down to the bus stop. All that marks the spot is a faded and dented sign. There used to be a bench, but a bunch of neighborhood kids destroyed it a couple of Halloweens back. So, I stand and wait, leaning my back against a half-naked walnut tree.

By the time the bus finally slows to a stop, the clear skies of the morning have started to shift to the cloudy, thick, gray blur of fall. I can see my breath in the air and my fingers and toes are numb. It must be somewhere in the mid-thirties right now. Yesterday had been so warm. I guess I should have listened to the meteorologist this morning. I make a mental note to dig through the totes in the garage and find my winter gear. A pair of gloves would have been nice today.

The bus is crowded for a Tuesday morning. I hate riding the bus when it's so full. Worse still, it seems like most of the passengers are traveling alone. That means there aren't many available seats to take unless I want to sit next to someone else, which I definitely do not. I crane my neck and scan the rows of faded cushions until I spot an empty space in the far back.

That's good. I prefer to ride in the back, anyway.

The old man at the wheel rolls his eyes at me frustratedly because I am taking too long, so I hold up my pass for his inspection. He knows that I take this bus almost every day, but he's a stickler for the rules. Last summer, he caught me eating a bag of Cheetos after work and gave me a very stern talking to. I don't eat on the bus anymore. He's never overly pleasant, but as long as I follow the rules, he usually leaves me alone. I appreciate that. I'm not generally in a talking mood.

The driver waves me by and pulls the lever to shut the doors behind me. The bus lurches into motion before I've made it to my seat, leaving me bumping and bobbing my way through the aisle. Several of the passengers stare as I pass, but I keep my eyes fixed on the ground.

I don't have to hallucinate their stares. They're always staring. Everyone around here knows who I am. I'm the freak that doesn't belong.

My cheeks heat with embarrassment, but I make it to the back and scrunch myself up in the seat. I can feel them watching me still, but I refuse to look back. Instead, I watch the bright leaves flash by as we hurtle toward town.

Damn, it would be nice to be allowed to drive.

THE BEST PART about my job is that people leave me alone. No one cares if I listen to my music as long as it isn't loud enough to disturb the peace. There's usually enough shelving and sorting to occupy my time. If there isn't, I have small projects like repairing broken bindings or setting up displays to keep me busy.

Books make good company. Books don't judge. They wait patiently to be judged by others.

I enter the back room and stow away my things before heading to the huge black canvas bin under the chute where the returned books fall. Sometimes I have company during the sort, but not today. Usually, my shifts line up with another girl near my age named Lauren, but she had a baby three weeks ago, so she'll be on maternity leave for a while.

I like Lauren. She has a nice smile, and she might think I'm weird, but she never says anything cruel. I don't mind her absence, though. I can move at my own pace when I work alone.

I roll the bin away from the chute and replace it with an empty one, then haul the mostly full one to the rickety table and begin to sort. Today, most of the books are for the Children's Room, and there are several smaller stacks for Adult Fiction, Teen, and Nonfiction, too.

I swipe my ID badge to access the computer system and use the handheld scanner to mark each one as returned before slipping them onto a small rolling cart. Once the counter is cleared, I push the much lighter bin back into the procession and roll my cart out onto the floor.

It takes nearly two hours to sort the books back into the stacks. That's fine with me. I like busy work. It doesn't leave me time to get lost in my head. When the cart is finally empty and all of the books have found their homes on the shelves, I search for something else to do.

My Halloween display is already finished, and there aren't any books set aside for repairs, so I decide to check with the manager to see what needs doing next. I slip through the door to the back room where the schedule is posted. Running my finger down the line, I stop when it lands on the afternoon square. The name "Nicky" is scribbled there. That's not the manager I was hoping for. Not at all. Anyone else would be better, in fact.

I close my eyes and prepare myself for an unpleasant interaction. Nicky has never been very fond of me. The feeling is certainly mutual.

My knuckles rap lightly on her office door. From inside, her chair squeaks as she straightens up and shuffles papers around.

"Come in," she calls.

I open the door and step inside.

"Ah, Selena. To what do I owe this pleasure?"

"I... uh," I say, trying to sound polite.

"Spit it out. I don't have all day."

Be professional. Don't get annoyed. It's only a short conversation.

"The first round of returns are processed," I finish. I hate when she interrupts me. Sometimes it takes me a little longer to put my thoughts together. She's rarely patient enough to wait.

"And?" she asks with a huff.

"And, I wanted to know if you had any priority projects today before I start something on my own. I don't want to mess things up if you have something planned."

"Honestly, Selena. If I had any priority projects, don't you think I would have taken care of them myself?"

"I don't know. Sometimes managers get busy."

"Yes, well. Currently, I'm busy wasting my time discussing this nonsense with you."

"Sorry..." I trail off. There are a whole lot of things that I want to say, but none of them would be workplace appropriate. I like this job. I don't want to lose it. So, I keep my mouth shut.

"Sorry doesn't give me back the time you've wasted." At this, she huffs again. "Go make sure the shelves are in order. Start with nonfiction tonight. Let's say 100-199. After that, cover 200-299, too." Don't bother me until it's finished."

Wow. That's pretty targeted. She's sending me to the Psychology and Religion sections. *Nice.* At best, it's thinly veiled discrimination. At worst, it's meant to get a rise out of me. Selena the Schizo. That's what she calls me behind my back.

I won't let her get to me today.

"I'll head right over," I answer coolly. "Are you sure you don't need anything else?"

"I need you to get out of my office and let me do my work. Clear?"

I need that, too.

"Crystal," I answer. Without another word, I walk out and shut the door behind me. Clenching my fists to quell the frustration barely beneath the surface, I walk away as quickly as I can, muttering under my breath. "I may be Selena the Schizo, but you're Nicky the Narcissist."

I say a few other choice words, too. Those don't warrant repeating.

Nonfiction is the least browsed section in our catalog. Most of our patrons are teens and moms with minivans full of tiny humans. Every once in a while, we get a college student with a research paper or an old man who loves to read about trains or cars. So, I'm not surprised to find the stacks empty.

I survey them carefully, checking to make sure the books are not just in the correct section, but also in the correct order. Most of them are. I pull the few that don't belong and make a neat pile on the floor, rearranging the others as needed. When I get to the section on Schizophrenia, I pause.

I've read quite a few of these myself. I wanted to understand what's wrong with me.

My fingers trail along the spines, stopping at a familiar volume: *A Study of Schizophrenia Emergence in Youth* by Sandra Holland, MD, Ph.D.

This book is about me.

I hate that Dr. Holland's book is on this shelf. My parents gave her permission to write about my case while I was still in the facility. That's how we found her after Dr. Branson left. They didn't see the problem with it because she swore she would only refer to me as some variation of "the patient" throughout her book.

She doesn't mention me by name, but anyone in this town who reads her study will know exactly who it's about. How many ten-year-old girls experience psychological breaks in the form of vicious demonic attacks? How many were found completely incoherent in their best friend's basement? How many thought that they had died and been resurrected?

It doesn't take a genius to put those things together and come up with my name.

I pull it down from the shelf and examine the crisp pages. It's in good shape. It hasn't been read often. But, there are enough fingerprint smudges to prove that at least a few people have picked it up. That doesn't surprise me. I'm an oddity in this town, a fascination. It's disgusting, but there's nothing I can do.

I'm not one for censorship, but I wish I could take this one with me and burn it.

I tuck the book back into its place on the shelf and walk away, taking the small pile of misfit books with me.

At least I can find them somewhere to belong. I don't think I'll ever belong here.

Nicky avoids me for the rest of my shift, and that's perfectly fine with me. When eight o'clock rolls around, I eagerly wrap myself up in my jacket and collect my things. I don't even wait to see if she has anything else for me to do. I'm over this place right now. I just want to get home to my comfortable pajamas and leftovers. Maybe I'll even read a little something of my own.

The evening air is much colder than it had been this afternoon. As predicted by the meteorologist, wind whips through the town and whistles between the buildings. I cross my arms and hold them close to my chest as I make my way down the four blocks to the bus stop. This one has a glass enclosure. I'll be able to stave off the chill as I wait safely inside.

The street is mostly empty. Only a few stragglers are making their way to the little tavern on the corner. There's not generally much bustle on a Tuesday evening. Most people want to go home, not roam aimlessly through town.

I'm about to step into the enclosure when something abruptly stops me. That's when I hear the dog.

A fog has formed in the narrow alley between two of the larger buildings across the way. I wouldn't think anything of it - we get a lot of fog this time of year - except somewhere hidden inside, I hear the high-pitched whimpers of a pet in need.

Generally, I'm not a fan of dogs. I have enough nightmares about them to leave me quite uneasy in their presence. But, this one sounds hurt. I can't just leave it there.

"Hello?" I call out. "Is anyone missing their dog? I think I found it."

No one answers.

I edge closer to the alley entrance, straining my eyes in a futile attempt to see the poor thing. It's no use. There are no lights in the alley, and the long days of summer have given in to the short days of fall. There's no lingering sunlight to help me at all.

I peer behind me, hoping that someone might be coming, but the street is empty. There's no one to help the dog but me.

So, shoving my fear down, I step into the swirling dark.

"Here, doggy," I call. My hands skim along one side of the alley to steady myself in the darkness. Thankfully, it appears that this alley is well tended to. There's no trash or broken pavement to trip over. Still, I move slowly.

"I won't hurt you. I'm here to help. Here, doggy..."

The whimper sounds again from a few feet away.

I take a couple more tentative steps and reach out my hand, stretching my fingers. They sweep across something bristly, coarse. The feeling is uncomfortable. It reminds me of touching my dad's grill brush. I pull my hand away.

"Is that you?" I ask, uncertain. "Dog?"

"Selena."

A hoarse whisper calls my name. I freeze, unable to move my feet that have rooted themselves into the ground.

"Selena. Fresh meat. Play with Selena. Rip. Claw. Devour, Selena."

"What the —"

I'm cut off abruptly when only inches in front of my face, glowing red eyes burst into view, faintly illuminating the space. They narrow and blink, moving as though a creature is tilting its head slowly from side to side.

Suddenly, I'm assaulted by a foul smell. I gag as the scent of rotten eggs and hot trash fills my nostrils. It's horrible. I have never smelled anything as disgusting as this.

I stumble backward, tripping over my own feet. The fog begins to clear as I do, revealing a huge, hulking form.

It's a dog, but it's not. Along its spine is a ridge of sharp spikes. The beast's fur is matted with blood, forming large clumps on its sides. Patches of its flesh are missing. Shockingly white bones pierce through rotting skin and muscle. Rows of razor-sharp teeth gleam in its mouth. Thick foam drips down onto the alley below. When it touches the pavement, the ground sizzles.

As I back farther away from the hideous creature, trying to put distance between myself and its deadly jaws, Dr. Holland's voice sounds in my head.

I remind myself to breathe. The more space I put between myself and the grotesque figure, the lighter the air becomes. I train my eyes on the dog's. It snaps its mouth and digs at the ground, leaving deep gouges in the pavement. A low rumble issues from deep within its chest.

This isn't real, Selena. It isn't real. This is just another hallucination. It's like the footsteps, but I can see it right in front of me. I just have to adjust my perception, that's all. I have to focus on what's real and what isn't. It's been a very stressful day today. This is all in my head, my mind's way of processing things beyond my abilities.

I blow out a slow breath and pause, staring at the horrific image.

"Selena. Selena. She wants to play. She wants me to chase. I want to chase. Such fun in the hunt. She stinks of fear. Delicious, girl. Devour."

"You're not real!" I yell, asserting myself and trying to force my will into reality. "You're not real. You're in my head. I'm not afraid of you! You're just a hallucination!"

A grinding, ear-splitting sound issues from the beast's

throat. If I didn't know better, I would say that it's laughing at me.

"You're not real!" I yell again, taking a step forward as if I can intimidate the thing into disappearing.

The beast moves so quickly that I barely register it. Huge, sharp claws send chunks of pavement flying as it darts directly for me. I gasp, and all thoughts of what's real and what's not disappear from my mind. Survival instinct kicks in.

Without thinking, I bolt out of the alley and race up the street, screaming for help as loudly as I can. The beast follows right at my heels, snapping and swatting at my back. I round a corner, and another, and one more, before colliding head-on with another person. He tries to steady me, but I send him sprawling to the ground. I land painfully beside him.

"Watch out!" I wail. "The dog... It's right behind me!"

The young man's face scrunches in confusion.

"The dog?"

"The dog! There's something wrong with it. I don't know. It's chasing me through the streets. Please, help. I..."

My eyes flick down the way that I came.

The street is empty. There's nothing there.

"No... It was just... It was just there. It was right there. You have to believe me. Please..."

"Umm, okay?"

Clearly, he doesn't.

I scramble up off of the cold ground and turn in circles, listening and watching. I wait to hear the heavy beats of its massive feet or smell that awful scent, but it doesn't come.

The young stranger picks himself up, too. He watches me closely as he dusts off his pants.

"Listen, if you need help..."

It takes everything I have to hold back my sobs.

"I can call an ambulance. Or, maybe your parents or something? Do you need me to call someone?"

I stare at him, shock numbing my emotions.

"No, I..." I cram my hands into the pockets of my jacket and squeeze them so tightly that my nails dig sharply into my palms. "I'm fine. I'm sorry. It was dark, and I guess... I was just confused."

He studies me, letting his eyes rove over my face.

"Wait, aren't you Selena?"

Anger fills me, warming me from head to toe and replacing my numbness as quickly as it came.

"That's none of your business," I snap. Turning abruptly on my heel, I march away toward the bus stop.

Behind me, I hear him mutter, "Freaking lunatic. Wow."

Hot tears run down my cheeks, leaving wet streaks for the cold wind to dry.

It wasn't real. I knew better.

I'll never live this one down.

CHAPTER FIVE

It isn't often that I get the couch all to myself on a weeknight. Usually, Dad watches his games and Mom sits at the island grading papers. I tend to prop myself up with a good book or write in my journal alongside them. But tonight, the living room is all mine.

After everything that happened with today's awful hallucinations, I'm thankful to be in control of my environment. I pop some movie theater butter popcorn and flick through the channels until I find reruns of one of my favorite shows. I stretch out and cover myself with Mom's cable-knit throw. It's heavy and soothing. It makes me feel safe.

I just want to feel safe.

I know I should go to bed, but I'm not ready to sleep yet. I don't want the whispers to return and torture me through the night. So instead, I munch on my popcorn until the large glass bowl is empty.

With greasy fingers and heavy eyes, I decide to take a

relaxing bath. I showered just this morning, I know, but I need something to calm me enough to lull me to sleep. I really do want to try what Dr. Holland suggested again, sleeping without the pills. If she says it's the right thing to do, then I at least owe her a solid attempt. That won't happen if I'm this high-strung. I have to try to knock myself out some other way.

My tiny bathroom doesn't have much, but it does have a small tub. Mom insisted on installing it with the remodel after I came home from the facility. She told my dad that every woman needs her own place of relaxation, and since my loft doesn't have a door and is missing the fourth wall, my privacy and opportunities for secluded relaxation are limited. This is the space meant just for me.

The scent of lavender fills the room as I pour a healthy scoop of Epsom salt under the faucet. I watch as the clear water rises. When it reaches the halfway mark, I peel off my clothes, toss them into the corner, and step inside. The heat feels perfect on my skin. I allow myself to sink down into it, breathing in the calming smell.

I don't need to scrub this time. I'm not dirty. I just need to lay back and close my eyes.

I imagine myself somewhere tropical, a shallow little lagoon. I swirl my hands through the water, letting the liquid slip languidly between my fingers. I picture the vibrant blue of the water and try to feel the enticing breeze on my skin. I slip down farther, dipping my face beneath the surface. The water caresses my cheeks and eyes.

It's peaceful, exactly what I needed.

Until long, thin fingers grab ahold of my shoulders and squeeze.

My eyes pop open, immediately stinging from the salt. I scream, but I'm still beneath the water, so all that escapes me are muffled cries. Air bubbles race to the surface, clouding my vision. The hands push me down until my head bounces off the bottom of the tub. A sharp pain zings through my skull, and I am momentarily disoriented.

I blink and use my arms to push against the tub's hard surface. The hands that hold me down are strong, but with enough effort, I manage to break free. I whip around, hair flailing wildly and spraying the room with water, expecting to see someone there. More water splashes out of the tub onto the blue tile floor, leaving a large puddle beside me.

Maybe I hadn't imagined the footsteps this morning. Whoever this is must have been lying in wait for hours, watching for the perfect moment to strike when my guard was finally down.

I push myself toward the spout and clear the water from my eyes, immediately scanning the small space.

There's no one there.

I'm speechless. This is so not funny. I don't understand why my mind is torturing me like this. It's not fair. I want to punch something or throw something. I just want to scream. And, since I am completely alone and there's no one to judge me, I do.

"Knock it off!" I screech. "I'm not playing this little game. It isn't real! Jesus, just leave me alone!"

Silence. I don't know what I expected. I'm the only one in the house.

Exasperated, I push my hair back out of my eyes. I can't catch a break.

I'm so tired. So very, very tired.

I turn around and lay back against the tub once more. I close my eyes and breathe deeply, trying to calm down.

That's when I hear the whispers again.

"Oh, Selena. Jesus won't help you," a woman's soft voice croons.

The water around me bursts into motion. Bubbles roil from the depths of the tub, and the temperature shoots up until the heat scalds me. Huge red welts appear on my skin as I launch myself over the edge, dragging my soaking-wet body across the cold tile floor. I slip and slide through the puddle as I make for the door.

The woman's too familiar cold laughter fills the room. I wrap my hand around the knob, but it won't turn. Terrified, I pull and kick, desperate to get away. It doesn't budge.

Behind me, the boiling water sloshes and gurgles. I press my head against the door and scream, unable to control my emotions and unwilling to look back. The impossible hands grab at my shoulders once more, tugging me toward the tub.

I resist as much as I can, but there's nothing to grab onto. They dig into my shoulders and spin me around. I whimper and keep my eyes shut, not wanting to see whatever horrific thing has touched my skin.

The sounds of the boiling water immediately stop. Silence, total and absolute, fills the room.

Shock propels me to open my eyes once more.

The tub is perfectly still. There's no creature in the room poised to attack. There's only the puddle on the floor where I dragged myself out of the tub and a trail of water to where I now sit, huddled against the bathroom door.

Frustration and fear spill out of me. A rage-filled howl escapes my chest.

"Why me?" I ask. "What did I do to deserve this? Why me?"

Wiping my eyes and nose, I pick myself up, careful not to slip on the mess I've made. I wrap myself in a towel and warily pull the plug.

The water drains.

Mesmerized and stunned, I stand there and stare.

I clean up the mess as quickly as I can.

With a heavy sigh, I grab my medication, sleeping pills included, and swallow the handful dry.

I can't do this anymore today. I just need to sleep. At this point, the nightmares will be a relief.

I sit on my bed and rock back and forth for a long while.

My grandma's old clock chimes one a.m. The sound echoes through the space and vibrates in my chest.

I'm hollow again. I'll have to try to be a better person tomorrow. Right now, I'm utterly numb.

OCTOBER 6TH

Today was ridiculously hard. I thought it would get better after my minor freak-out this morning. I was incredibly wrong.

I can't believe I embarrassed myself like that after work. That hallucination was so obvious. There are no real dogs like that. I should have known better than to let it get to me. And that poor guy. I hope he's okay. I was so mad when he figured out who I was that I didn't even bother to ask.

I'm literally the worst excuse for a human that ever existed. Who knocks someone to the ground like that and walks away?

Everyone thought I was nuts before. This is SO not going to help. I'm not only the girl who cried demon when she was ten — I'm the woman who cried monster-dog when she was twenty-eight, too!

And what the hell was that with the bath? I have never seen it do that before. Well, it didn't really do that. Did it? I felt how hot the water was, though. I felt hands touching me. My skin burned. But, it was fine when I opened my eyes. The water was calm, and the burns were completely gone.

I can't believe it's the first day that my parents have been away and I'm already such a mess. Like yeah, it's stressful that they're gone, but am I really this incompetent?

What are these meds even for if they can't keep this stuff from happening? Occasional small things like scary whispers I can understand, but these have been full-blown hallucinations. I'm not just hearing things. I'm seeing them, feeling them, smelling them...

It's so hard to tell what's real and what's not in the moment.

I haven't been this afraid in a long, long time.

I am going to have to talk to Dr. Holland.

Please don't let her send me back to the facility.

I won't go back there. Not again.

WEDNESDAY, OCTOBER 6TH

CHAPTER SIX

WEDNESDAY

THE TWINKLING MELODY OF MY NINE A.M. ALARM ASSAULTS MY EARS far too soon. I'm not ready to be awake. I'm sure that my eyes have only been shut for a matter of minutes.

I glare at the phone on the nightstand beside me, remnants of heavy sleep clouding my vision. I blink and squint, trying to clear the blurriness away. It takes a second to orient my focus on the tiny white numbers that incessantly flash on the screen.

Yes, it's actually nine a.m. No, I'm not willing to wake up enough to roll over and shut it off.

My body feels stiff, and the bits of my legs and arms that slipped out from beneath my covers while I slept are entirely too cold for my liking. That doesn't bode well for abandoning my bed and acting like an adult. I'm comfortable in my little cocoon. I absolutely will not be comfortable outside of it. I'm not ready to face these chillier autumn temperatures.

Silently, I chastise myself for not turning up the heat before falling asleep last night. That wasn't smart, especially since I don't even have to go all the way down to the thermostat to do it. Everything is Bluetooth controlled now. I could have done it from the comfort of my bed. I really need to start thinking things through.

Then again, I had other things on my mind. You know, like being boiled alive in my own bathtub, or maybe mauled to death by a demon dog, or that woman's voice... that strangely familiar voice.

A shiver having nothing to do with the cool air passes over me. Keeping as much of myself under the warm blanket as I can, I pull my phone over to myself by the cord and shut off the obnoxious alarm, then I shove my head beneath the covers and clutch them tighter to my body, snuggling back into the pocket of warmth between my blankets and my mattress.

I can't help but feel like a small child tucked away in my little bubble. I don't remember much of my childhood. Dr. Holland has told me over and over again that forgetting things is a typical response to significant trauma. What I do remember tends to be unsettling, but there are a few sweet moments hidden away here and there. Being bundled in my bed reminds me of when I used to have nightmares. I would cry out and wake my parents, but neither of them ever complained. Dad brought me a glass of water, and Mom snuggled up next to me and played with my hair until my eyes grew heavy again. Before going back to bed, she used to tell me that my blanket was a magic shield, that with my blanket, nothing bad could ever touch me. She would cover up my little hands and feet, then tuck my blanket underneath me. Then, she'd kiss my forehead and tell me goodnight again before leaving the room.

I'm sure I looked like a child trapped in a little vacuum-sealed package, but it helped me more than she will ever know. Ever since, I've kept my magic blanket close. Even in the heat of summer, I won't go to bed without it. It was with me in the treatment center, and it's wrapped around me now.

Of course, I know that the blanket isn't really a magical shield. It's just a blanket. The only protection it provides is a false sense of security. There are scarier things that hide in the dark than the childhood boogeyman that frequented my dreams. There are actual, real-life demons waiting to maim and murder innocent little girls. No amount of blanket will ever keep them at bay.

No, stop it. Demons aren't real.

I know demons aren't real. I'm not starting down that path, not after yesterday. That's asking for more panic and hallucinations. I refuse to be that person. I won't let my imagination win.

I wait for sleep to claim me again, but it doesn't come. Even though I'm tired, I'm not used to getting this much rest. My parents make enough noise in the morning to wake the neighbors, and without a closed-in space of my own, I can't block them out and go back to sleep, no matter how hard I try. It's always pots and pans, the morning news, or Dad scrambling to find his watch and keys. I had hoped that with the house empty, going back to sleep might be easier to do, but I guess old habits die hard.

Even though I'm still tired, I actually slept well last night, too. That isn't helping my cause. After how much stress and chaos I endured yesterday, I expected my dreams to be riddled with monstrous dogs and insidious creatures, but to my happy surprise, I don't remember dreaming at all.

Honestly, I can't remember the last time I had a dreamless night. I'm so glad I gave in and took the sleeping pills. Maybe Dr. Holland is wrong about them. Maybe they do help? I don't know. I'll have to talk with her about it tomorrow.

My alarm rings again ten minutes later. I thought I turned it off, but I must have hit the snooze.

"Alright, you win," I complain. I reach for my phone and shut the alarm off completely this time, then turn up the heat before swatting away my blanket. I let out a yawn, then stand and walk to the bathroom to get ready for the day.

When I reach the door, I pause. Hesitating, my hand hovers over the knob. Logic tells me that what happened last night wasn't real, that it was all in my head. Still, an irrational part of me doesn't want to go inside. What if it *was* real and not some screwed-up hallucination? Neither option is ideal. Either I have suddenly developed a tolerance to my many medications and my sanity is slipping or there's a terrifying being hiding behind the door, waiting to rip me to shreds when I finally pull it open.

I don't know which one is worse, really...

Slowly, I twist the knob. The door opens with a quiet click, swinging back into the dark space. I fumble with the switch and turn on the overhead light.

Quickly, my eyes rove over the tiny space. There are no puddles on the floor. I cleaned those up. The bathtub is not filled with impossible boiling water. In fact, there's no water at all. I pulled the plug and watched it drain last night. There's no ghoul staring at me hungrily from the corner. But, what did I really expect to find?

I'm losing my mind. Again.

The heavy weight of defeat sinks into my stomach as I step inside and get ready for my day.

AN IDEA STRIKES me as I take out last night's braid. I have no clue if it's a good idea, but it's an idea nonetheless.

Aside from the constant judgment and the social isolation, the hardest part about living with crippling hallucinations is not knowing what's real and what isn't. I haven't had episodes like this in a very long time. Actually, I don't remember things being this bad since I was admitted to the facility. But, they're bad now. Very, very bad.

I'm used to the whispers. They bother me, sure, but they aren't as bad as the things I have been seeing and feeling for the last twenty-four hours. These hallucinations aren't just terrifying, but frustrating. I need a way to know if the things I see are real or simply messed-up projections of my imagination.

So, that's where my plan comes in.

Rifling through the bins in my closet, I search for my little plastic camera. It's one of the modern ones that mimics old-school Polaroids. You take a picture and it somehow shows up on these thick prints that pop right out of the camera itself. You have to shake them for a little while. I always loved the idea of that part. But, once you're done shaking them, the pictures are right there in front of you, perfect replicas of the thing you tried to capture.

I'm going to find that camera and its film, and I'm going to carry that around with me today. If I see something, I'll snap a picture. If it's not on the little print, I'm hoping that means it's not real. I have no idea if this will work, but if it does, it will save me a lot of trouble. Plus, I'll have pictures to take to my therapy session tomorrow so that Dr. Holland and I can talk all of this through.

Yeah, I really hope that this works.

When my fingers wrap around the teal camera, a sense of relief washes over me. I pull it down and inspect it, checking to make sure that it still functions. Everything seems fine, so I continue my search for the small box of film. This I find in good condition, too. I smile at my ingenious little tools. Maybe things are starting to go my way today.

It's been a long time since I used a real camera to take a picture. I think the last serious picture I took was of the tree-house. My eyes flick to my copy of the image, an exact replica of the other one hanging in Dr. Holland's office. I'm honestly not sure if I've even used this camera for more than a few test shots. It seemed so cool when I bought it, but that was before I realized that most of the people who used cameras like these did so with their friends, and I don't have any of those. I'm pretty sure the day that I realized how lonely I really was is the exact same day that I hid the camera away in the back of my closet. I didn't need any more proof that my life is a hot mess.

At least it has a purpose now.

I turn the camera to face myself and snap a picture, testing it out. The photo slides out quickly, dropping into my open hand. A few minutes later, after shaking the image and watching it slowly appear in the square, I'm holding a clear picture of myself: wavy blonde hair from sleeping with a wet braid, light green eyes, a small nose, and a sad little smile.

It works well enough, I guess. I toss the picture onto my nightstand.

I don't have therapy today, and I don't have to go to work. I have no plans whatsoever. I turn the camera over and over in my hands, trying to decide how to use my free time. I could read a new book, but that's what I always do. Not that there's anything wrong with reading, of course. There's a reason I work at the library, after all. I guess I could rent a movie, but I'm not really in the mood to sit still. I have so much nervous energy stored up from yesterday that I need to burn off. I want to do something different.

I'm surprised when I realize that I want to leave the house. Generally, I'm a bit of a homebody. Home is much more comfortable, away from prying eyes and judgmental whispers. I don't want to be cooped up, though. I feel the need to explore. The problem is, I really don't want to be around people. If yesterday was any indication, being around others might only further solidify the notion that I've lost my marbles. Strangers tend to shy away from the panicked girl running down the street and babbling about invisible monsters. I can't blame them. If I was well enough to tell the difference, it would probably freak me out, too.

No, as much as I want to get out of the house, today is not the day to try to make friends.

But, where can I go then? Not town, obviously. That's where the people are. I need somewhere quiet, somewhere within walking distance so that I don't have to ride the bus, but far enough away that I will be able to purge myself of this feeling, this manic energy buzzing in my veins.

Then it hits me: I could take a short hike and settle myself down. Maybe I could go back to the abandoned treehouse. The last time I took a good picture with a real camera was when I found myself there.

As this thought settles in, I feel a strange pull in my stomach. It's like my body already knew where it wanted to go this entire time and my mind is only now catching up with the truth.

I can't see why I shouldn't go to the treehouse. I don't think it belongs to anyone anymore. I don't even think it was built on anyone's property. It's just there, out in the woods. That's a solid bonus. I probably won't run into anyone on my way. After all, why would anyone else bother traipsing through the woods in the middle of the day?

Tugging the lanyard of the little teal camera up over my

head and dropping it on like a necklace, I stick the box of film into my hoodie pocket. Trying to be responsible, I keep my promise to eat. Mom's lasagna is even better as leftovers, and despite not really being a breakfast food, I don't regret a single bite as I clean my plate. I rinse my dish and throw on my coat and a pair of worn tennis shoes before slipping outside into the crisp air and heading for the trees.

I SHOULD BE USED to the feeling of being watched by now, but I'm not sure it's something I'll ever learn to live with. It isn't necessarily terrifying, not like the things that happened yesterday, but it is unsettling. I can't see anything out of place or hear anyone else nearby. Still, there's an ever-present sense that someone's eyes are boring into my back no matter which way I turn.

It's nice to be out of the house, though. Somehow, the air inside the house felt stale and the space was too stifling. None of it makes sense. It should feel bigger with fewer people inside. It doesn't. It feels smaller, like the walls are pushing in on me. Out here, the air may be chilly, but it's fresh, and with all of nature at my back, there's plenty of room to breathe.

Leaves crunch beneath my feet as I skirt fallen branches. There used to be a path here, I think. If it's still there, it's buried beneath the destruction caused by the recent strong winds. The leaves are slick and smell of new decay. The scent is raw and earthy, not entirely unpleasant. I let myself succumb to the slight burning in my calves and thighs as I kick the leaves aside, following the pull in my stomach deeper and deeper into the woods.

When my destination comes into view, I let out a sigh of

relief. I had been unconsciously worried that I wouldn't know where to find the treehouse again after all this time, but there it is, nestled between two thick branches of a walnut in the center of a bare patch of forest, that same tattered curtain blowing gently in the breeze.

I listen for the sounds of children hiding inside. There are none, so I carefully climb the broken ladder and pull myself up to the moss-slicked floor.

It's just as I remember it, if not a little worse for wear. There are a few more missing boards this time, and some of the drawings have faded away. For some reason, I'm struck with a sense of profound sadness. A place like this shouldn't be abandoned. *What happened to the happy kids who spent their days playing here?*

They're probably long gone, I muse. They've grown out of childhood and into other things. I wish I could have had a childhood like that - peaceful and happy.

My childhood memories were stolen from me. Sure, there are small moments like riding the school bus or throwing up from the stomach flu. But, there are so many things that just aren't in my head. I don't remember birthdays, or playing with friends, or sleepovers, or ice skating at the town rink. My parents claim that I did all of those things and more.

I didn't do all of that, though. It was her.

No, she doesn't exist. You did those things. You just don't remember. It's because of your broken mind.

I sigh and slide down onto the floor, careful to avoid the holes forming near the walls from years of rot. Like before, I hold up my camera and snap a picture of the space. I have no idea why. Honestly, I don't understand why I came here in the first place. This was probably a mistake, a waste of time. I should have left this sad skeleton alone.

A leaf skitters across the floor and bumps into my hand, so

I scoop it up and twirl it between my fingers. The flashes of red and yellow are beautiful. I contemplate taking it with me, but that would be silly. It doesn't belong in my house. It belongs here in the woods where it can contribute to something. It needs to turn to mulch and fertilize the plants or feed the fungi. Instead of keeping it, I reach over and slip my hand through a large rectangular opening. I let the leaf drop out of the window, drifting lazily to the ground below.

As I turn back and prepare to stand, something in the corner catches my eye.

I reach for it, only to find that it's a small, red, metal box, rusted with age.

"What are you?" I ask as I pull it closer. There's a space for a lock, but if there was one, it has long since been discarded, so I lift up the lid and poke around inside. An old rag doll sits on the top, covered in dirt and grime. It looks as though it was well-loved in its time. Beneath the doll is a tiny porcelain tea set and a half-used sketchbook. Underneath these treasures is a photograph.

Confusion settles over me as I stare at the faces of two little girls. At first, I don't recognize them at all. One has straight, mousey brown hair, and the other has a head of bobbed golden blonde. The blonde girl is taller, maybe older, but the brunette stands on her tiptoes with her arm around the other girl's waist. They're happy, smiling from ear to ear. They look like the best of friends. These must be the girls who played up here when this place was in better shape, many years ago.

As I study the image, something about them begins to look familiar.

I notice her eyes first, then the one tooth that isn't quite lined up with the rest. The freckles across her nose and the sunburn on her forehead make the color of her eyes pop.

Alexandria. That little girl is Alexandria Hendricks. She's the one that my mom claims was my childhood best friend. She's the one whose basement I...

My thoughts trail off as I realize who the little girl beside her is. It's me. This picture is of Alexandria Hendricks and me. But, that's not possible.

I have absolutely no memories of Alexandria from before the day of the incident. I don't remember playing with her as a child. I don't remember hugging her, or having tea parties, or playing with dolls, or climbing the ladder to this treehouse...

This is an impossible picture.

I'm an impossible person.

Yet, here it is. It's in my hand, as solid as the picture I took in this dilapidated place only moments ago.

I lift my own picture up and examine it beside the one from the box, shaking my head in disbelief.

I was here. I played with Alexandria. That's why my body knew where to go. That's why I felt the call to the treehouse in the first place.

Why can't I remember any of this? Why does my childhood have to be so full of holes? No one believes my story. None of this makes any sense at all.

I rip the picture in half and discard it among the piles of leaves, then rip up my own, furious at myself for coming here. I should have known better than to leave the house and go out into the world. Home, therapy, and work. Those are the places I belong. I don't belong in the middle of the woods in a godforsaken treehouse.

Eyes full of tears, I practically jump down the ladder and retrace my steps until I make it home. I'm not leaving here again today. I'm sticking with the tried and true, books and old movies until it's time for bed.

THE REST of the day passes in a depressing blur. When night falls, I'm thankful for the darkness. At least I have a reason to sleep.

I wash my face in the bathroom sink and brush my teeth, then study my reflection in the mirror. The sad face of a lost little girl, all grown-up and incredibly alone, stares back at me. I grab my camera and snap a picture of myself standing in front of the mirror. Maybe I'll bring this shot to Dr. Holland's office, too. I'll call it "the girl who doesn't belong."

I scoop up my meds and swallow them down, then lean forward against the sink until my forehead touches the mirror.

I'm so tired. I'm so very, very tired of being so completely alone.

A subtle movement in the reflection catches my eye, so I look up. As usual, there's nothing there. But, there's something about my eyes that I don't recognize, a faint red ring around my iris. I bring my hand up to my face and gently pull back my eyelid to examine it closer.

"Weird," I whisper as I move my head from side to side and stare at my own reflection.

I just need sleep, I tell myself. *Whatever it is will go away in the morning.*

I'll take an extra sleeping pill tonight. I just need some rest. Dr. Holland will sort me out tomorrow. Tomorrow is a new day.

The pills kick in fast, and I'm too groggy to write in my journal, so I crawl into bed and use my phone to turn off the lights. It takes only seconds for the vast emptiness to drag me down into oblivion.

THURSDAY, OCTOBER 7TH

CHAPTER SEVEN

LATE THURSDAY MORNING

"How has it been with your mom and dad out of town? Are you doing alright?" Her patient eyes bore into me, and though I know she's on my side, I shrink into myself anyway.

"I've been better." I hug the sequin pillow tight to my chest like a shield. She waits patiently for me to continue, but I know that my defensiveness has not gone unnoticed.

"How so?"

I don't want to answer this question. Instead, I let my mind wander, fixating on anything else in the room. I settle on the smell. Dr. Holland's office smells like cinnamon. She always chooses scents that relate to the season for the wax melter on her desk. I'm guessing it makes people feel more comfortable. This one reminds me of apple cider. It makes my mouth water. Suddenly, I'm thirsty.

"Do you have anything to drink?" I ask. It's an obvious stalling tactic.

Even though she knows that I'm avoiding our conversation, Dr. Holland places her notepad down on the little table beside her chair and rises without a word. I look away. I'm embarrassed that this is so hard to talk about.

Why is it so hard to talk about, anyway? She's my therapist. That's what I came here to do, to talk. I should just talk.

She cracks the seal on a tiny bottle of water and hands it to me before returning wordlessly to her seat and picking up the notepad once more.

"Thanks."

"Of course."

The water is cold, and it helps a little. It's no substitute for apple cider, though. I make a note to pick some up from the store. God, I'm still stalling. What's wrong with me? So many things...

"So, why don't you tell me about what's going on?"

Thoughts race through my mind, everything that has happened since my parents left. First, the invisible footsteps, then the demon dog, then the spindly hands and the boiling bath. And the picture...

I fidget with the sequins, flipping them over and back again. What am I supposed to say? "I've suddenly lost the ability to tell the difference between reality and my imagination again, but don't worry, my mom left me plenty of lasagna?" Yeah, that will go over splendidly.

No, I have to approach this carefully. I need to tell her the truth, but I have to phrase it in a way that doesn't make it sound like I'm incapable of taking care of myself without my parents.

I start by keeping it simple and say, "I've been hallucinating again."

Dr. Holland leans against the back of her chair and tucks the one section of gray hair on the side of her head back behind her ear. A slight look of concern settles on her usually pleasant face. "What kind of hallucinations have you had, Selena?"

It's funny. I've been coming here for all these years, and she's been carefully studying me, but apparently, I've been studying her, too. I can see the way her eyes have narrowed slightly. Her focus has sharpened. This is a bigger problem than she's letting on, and I haven't even told her how severe the hallucinations have been.

Tread carefully, I remind myself. *She's not your friend. She's a doctor, and she can have you institutionalized if you screw this up.*

So, I start at the beginning. I choose my words carefully, trying not to let my fear show.

"It started pretty soon after mom and dad left. I was making myself breakfast, but then the power went out at the house. I fixed it, but it went out again. That was odd."

She scribbles in her notepad but says nothing.

"I think I was already stressed about mom and dad leaving, so when the power went out, it must have been enough to trigger me, you know?

"I can understand that," she answers. She cocks her head to the side slightly. "Continue, please."

"Well, when I was trying to fix the power, I heard footsteps up in my room. I wasn't sure that was what the sound was at first, but then I realized it sounded like someone pacing. I thought that there was someone in my house. It scared me."

"That would scare anyone, especially someone who isn't used to being alone."

I nod.

"What did you do next?"

Casting my mind back to that morning, I continue. "I grabbed my mom's baseball bat and went upstairs to investigate."

"That was very brave of you."

I don't respond to this. I didn't feel very brave in the moment.

"What did you find?"

"There was no one there."

She scribbles something else on the paper. "Do you think this might have been a reaction to your parents' absences? Perhaps you wished that you weren't home alone, so your mind inserted an auditory hallucination to fill the void?"

I don't like this response, not because she's way off the mark, but because it makes too much sense.

Am I really so desperate for company that I would create a terrifying hallucination just to feel like I'm not alone? After less than an hour?

I scour the moments leading up to the footsteps. I had been a little sad. I had been worried about being alone. The quiet had been unsettling... the quiet. Had I hallucinated the footsteps to fill the silence? But, I had the tv on. I had already filled the void another way. Then the power went out...

Confusion and embarrassment cause my eyes to water and sting. "Maybe," is all I can say. "But, why would my hallucination scare me like that? That doesn't make any sense. And, why would the footsteps come from my room? I wasn't in my room."

Dr. Holland's eyes wander through the office. She's lost in thought, much like I was only moments before. I can practically see the wheels turning in her mind before she flicks her eyes back to me.

"Maybe the sounds manifested as fear because your logical mind knew you were home alone, even though your emotions wished that you weren't. The part of you that wanted someone to be there with you knew that it wasn't possible, and when that contradiction arose, it didn't make sense. That dissonance could have resulted in fear."

"So, I sort of willed another person into existence for a moment, but I knew that wasn't possible, and I scared myself?"

"In essence. Does that seem likely?"

I hate that her analysis makes so much sense. It's only further proof that I'm losing my mind.

"Okay, but why would they be in my room?"

"Well, that could be because your room is your most familiar space. Or, perhaps it could be because your eyes couldn't see the manifestation that your mind created, so your mind simply placed the manifestation somewhere out of sight. There are a great many factors that come into play in situations such as this. I wish I could answer these questions with certainty for you, but unfortunately, I cannot."

"I know."

A heavy silence fills the space between us. I set the sequined pillow aside and tip my head back against the top of the couch, staring up at the ceiling tiles.

"Have you had any other hallucinations?"

"Yeah."

I refuse to look at her and see her concerned expression again. It will only make sharing that much harder.

"There was this dog in an alley after work the other night."

"A dog in an alley?"

"Mmhmm," I answer. "I saw it when I was on my way home. Well, I heard it first. It whimpered like it was hurt, and there was no one else around, so I went looking for it. I thought it needed my help."

"Dogs are often in alleys. At least, stray dogs are."

"That's what I thought when I heard it."

"So, this hallucination was auditory as well?"

"At first. Then, I found it. I'm not sure I can describe it correctly..." I trail off, picturing the beast.

"Take your time."

I pause, fidgeting with the sequins again.

"It looked like it was dead. I could see bones sticking out, and it was missing huge patches of fur. There was blood and an awful smell..."

"A smell?"

"Yeah, like rotting meat and eggs. Like, when you leave a bag of trash outside for too long in the heat? It smelled like that."

She clicks her pen and scribbles again.

"So, this time you not only heard the dog whining, but you saw and smelled the hallucination as well?"

"Yeah. It felt like it was real. Like, really real. Like it was right in front of me. I even touched it. Or, I think I did."

I look over at her only to find her lost in thought again.

After a few moments, she says, "Is it possible that what you found in the alley was an actual deceased dog?"

"It was definitely alive."

"It may have seemed that way. But, is it possible that what you saw saddened you or scared you enough that you imagined an alternative scenario, that the dog was actually alive despite its appearance and scent?"

Had I done that? The creature certainly seemed dead enough. Where would I have gotten those details? How could they have come from my mind?

"As we are both aware, you have always had a fear of dogs. Your nightmares are proof of that. It stands to reason then that you may have accidentally created this terrifying dog-like creature as a mixture of your own fear and unwillingness to accept such a sad scene. Could that be possible?"

"I guess." I blow out a shaky breath. "But, how would I know for sure? Have you heard anything about a dead dog?"

"I haven't, but that doesn't mean there hasn't been a dead dog in town. Accidents happen all the time. If the dog was a stray, it could have been hit by a car. You said it was in a dark alley. Perhaps a dog might have been injured or killed by a vehicle and left undiscovered for a time."

"Maybe." It's a possibility, but it was so real.

"I'll think about this particular hallucination, and we can get back to it at our next session if that's alright with you. I'd like to do a little research, find out if some of my theories may be correct.

"Okay."

"Have there been any more?"

"I felt hands push me down into my bath, and then I felt the water get super hot and saw it start to boil."

She scribbles again.

"And when I got out, the door wouldn't open. That's when I heard the woman laughing."

"The same woman from your nightmare?"

"I think so."

"And you're certain that you were awake?"

"I..." Defeat settles upon me once more. "I guess I could have fallen asleep in the bath. I thought I was awake. I don't know. I don't know..."

She scribbles a final note and sets her pen aside.

"You've been experiencing a lot of stress this week," she states, matter-of-factly. "That would be enough to cause anyone to struggle. Given your situation, there are mitigating circumstances that we have to consider. I'd like to make a few changes and see how that affects your hallucinations. Are you open to that?"

"If it will make them stop, absolutely."

"I can't guarantee anything, but we can certainly try. Let's increase some of your dosages for the time being. If it helps, that's great. If it doesn't, we can always lower them back down. Is that alright?"

"I guess."

"This is your treatment, Selena. We won't do anything that you don't want to do."

I don't want to increase the dosages. Some of the medications already make me feel numb. I can only imagine what higher doses will do. But, I really don't want to keep imagining more and more horrifying things until I lose my mind completely and hurt myself or someone else.

"It's fine."

"And I'd like to reassert that you should take a break from the sleeping pills. My guess is that you've been taking them because of the hallucinations, yes?"

She always knows.

"Yeah, sorry."

"There's no need to apologize in this room. I understand why you would feel the need to use them to escape the stress and fear. That's only natural, especially since you've relied on them for so long. But, I worry that they may be making matters worse. Try to avoid them for the time being, Selena. It could really help."

I nod my head again. I don't want to, but I'll try.

"And, I suspect you won't like this next suggestion."

"What?" I ask, bracing myself for the worst.

"I think you should cut out caffeine for a while."

"Why?" I protest, but she continues.

"Caffeine is a stimulant, and it seems that your mind is already overstimulated with your parents gone and the increase in hallucinations. You haven't experienced anything so severe in a long time. Besides, cutting out caffeine may help you rest without the sleeping pills. It's a good idea."

"No coffee?"

"No coffee. No caffeinated beverages or tea, either. And no chocolate."

I groan. *This absolutely sucks.*

"Just try it for a few days, okay?"

I can tell that I'm sulking like a sullen teenager, but I grimace and agree. "Fine."

"We can re-evaluate in a few weeks' time."

Weeks without caffeine? Ugh. I know she's trying to help. She's always trying to help, but this is going to be nearly impossible.

"Is there anything else you need to share?" she asks, returning to her cool, patient demeanor.

I rub my face with both of my hands and sigh. "Yeah, one more thing."

"Okay. Whenever you're ready."

I'm not ready for any of this. I'll never be ready for it. I don't tell her that, though. It won't do me any good. Instead, I tell her about the plan I concocted for my camera and my trip to the abandoned treehouse in the woods. I tell her about the picture that I found in the lockbox. I tell her about how unsettling it felt to hold proof that we were friends in my hand, and how I raced back home and shut out the rest of the world for the rest of the day.

She nods her head in all the right places and waits for me to finish before she says, "Why do you think you went back to that place?"

"I don't know," I answer truthfully. "Honestly, I have no idea."

"And, what do you remember of your time spent with Alexandria as a child?" she prods.

"Nothing. Absolutely nothing. We've talked about this before."

"I know. Sometimes, extenuating circumstances can bring repressed memories to the surface."

"I don't remember." I swirl my foot on the shag rug again,

retracing the familiar circular pattern I have perfected through so many sessions before.

"Most likely, that's a trauma response. Neither of us has a firm understanding of the events that led to your psychological break in Alexandria's basement when you were young. That's part of what we've been working toward all this time. So, I have an assignment for you, if you're willing."

Another one? Yay...

"I want you to go home tonight and write about how that picture made you feel. Really think about it. Let your mind and body still. Let yourself drift back into whatever memories you can find from your childhood. Write all of it down, and bring it with you to our next session. Can you do that?"

No. Absolutely not.

"Yeah, I'll try."

"Good. Good." She clears her throat. "I hate to end it here, but that's all the time we have for the day. Do you want me to schedule you for an evening appointment tomorrow, or should I see you again next week as planned?"

I scoot forward to the edge of the couch, ready to leap up and run from this office as quickly as I can.

"Next week is great, thanks."

"Next week it is. I'll call down to the pharmacy in just a moment to give them the new orders. You should pick up the medications on your way home. I'd like for you to start taking them tonight."

"Okay."

"And I like the idea you have of using your camera to ground yourself in reality. You should give it a try. The worst thing that happens is that it doesn't work and you've wasted a few pieces of film, right? Let yourself control your situation as best as you can. Agency is important. Remember, you are in charge of your life, not your hallucinations."

I nod. *I'm in charge.* It doesn't feel like I'm in charge. I repeat it over and over again in my head. *I'm in charge. I'm in charge. I'm in charge.*

Dr. Holland stands and performs her usual end-of-session ritual. She unlocks her desk and switches out notepads, then locks it again.

"I'll see you next week."

"I'll be here," I answer.

She politely dismisses me with a wave of her hand and a smile as she lifts her phone to her ear, probably calling the pharmacy already.

I don't need to be told twice. I'm gone.

Today's session was difficult. I hate difficult sessions. I'm leaving more frustrated than I was when I came in. At least I told her the truth, though. At least we're working on things. At least I'm not in this alone.

As the door to Dr. Holland's office clicks shut behind me, I accidentally make eye contact with the man Dr. Holland called Stanley at the end of my last appointment. He smiles sympathetically at me and says, "Rough one?"

"Yeah, you could say that," I answer. I turn away and make for the door.

"We've all been there," is all he says.

As I open the exterior door and step out into the midday sun, he waves politely and I wave back before turning my back to him and shoving my headphones into my ears.

The pharmacy is only five blocks away. I don't need the bus. I don't need anyone's stares. I need to walk, to get away.

A gust of wind blows me forward and I disappear into the music, letting my troubled mind fade away for a little while.

CHAPTER EIGHT

EARLY THURSDAY AFTERNOON

"Alright, Ms. Thomas. We'll have those prescriptions out for you shortly."

"Yeah, thanks," I say uncomfortably, not meeting the woman's eyes. Filling my prescriptions here is so awkward, too personal. I'd much rather order them online and have them delivered as usual. That's the easy way. Online pharmacies don't ask many questions. They don't care as long as the bill is paid.

I glance around the store at the few customers scattered throughout the aisles. It's not very busy right now, but that doesn't surprise me. Most of the usual customers are probably at work or at school. The people who *are* here pointedly look away when they make eye contact with me. They're trying to be inconspicuous. They're failing miserably.

I know they were watching and listening. To them, I'm strange, maybe even dangerous, a thing to be carefully monitored from afar. I'm probably the only person in this town that has to take antipsychotics. Everyone else is so incredibly "normal." I can't help but think that the labels on my pills only isolate me more. So, they treat me like the plague. Don't come close and it won't happen to you. Never mind that Schizophrenia isn't even contagious. Not even close.

The pharmacy technician follows my gaze but says nothing as she steps away from the counter and around to the back. There isn't anything to be said. We both know the truth.

I clear my throat and tuck my wallet into my pocket, trying to decide what I'll do to kill the time while I wait. Everyone else is wandering the aisles with their little green shopping baskets, buying things they probably don't even need. I decide it will be best to mimic them. It's better than wasting time sitting an an uncomfortable metal bench and staring at the wall. It's better than being a stoic spectacle, too.

So, I grab a basket and wander down the closest aisle. This one contains a host of clearance items and discount school supplies. Most of the things crammed onto the shelves have either been opened and returned or are no longer useful, like the old student planners that ended before the most recent school year even began. The pharmacy is hoping to squeeze out whatever pennies they can manage. I can't blame them in a small town like this. I'd bct that most people are like me. They get their prescriptions somewhere else and pick up their groceries from a big chain store. I bet every penny goes a long way when the customer pool is as shallow as a puddle.

Rounding the corner, I find myself in the snacks and drinks aisle. While the clearance section contained nothing of interest for me, this one is much more up my alley. I could use a little something sweet after that stressful session, and I'm still thirsty after the tiny, disappointing bottle of water.

No caffeine, though, I remind myself. I roll my eyes. That means no chocolate and no pop, two of my favorite treats. How incredibly boring. These weeks are going to be such a drag.

An older woman smiles apprehensively at me as she passes by, but I keep my eyes trained on the display of hanging bags, looking for anything suitable. The snack and candy selections are minimal, disappointing. I finally settle on a small bag of chips and package of gummy bears. Salty and sweet. These will have to do.

I drop these into my basket before moving along to the shelf-stable drinks. Coffee is off-limits now, and so are most of my favorite teas, but I manage to find a decently interesting, non-caffeinated option for later. I toss the box of tea into my basket beside the snacks, too.

Now that Dr. Holland has said I can't have any caffeine, caffeine is all that I want. That's always been one of my toxic traits. My mouth waters as I pass by the sugary drinks. I may not be able to drink pop for a little while, but I'm hoping they have something else.

My fingers are crossed as I move from door to door. It's October. They've got to have at least a little bit of apple cider. *Please let them have cider. Please, please, please.*

Luckily enough, they have a handful of child-sized bottles, so I snatch two of these and add them to the basket as well. At least one thing is working out for me today. One thing is good. It's a start.

I pop one of the containers open and sip it as I approach the register. Instant satisfaction makes me smile. It's cold, crisp, and perfectly sweet. There really is nothing in the world like cider. I'd drink an entire gallon if it wouldn't make me sick. It's the kind of drink worth waiting an entire year for.

The woman at the register gives me an odd look as I pile my little collection of junk on the counter. She looks from the small bottle in my hand to me and back, eyebrows high and unamused.

"Just killing time," I tell her as I take another sip.

Without a word, she takes my card and bags up my snacks and drinks.

By the time the pharmacist calls me back, I've finished off my scant junk food feast and am swallowing the last few drops of my precious drink. I toss the little bottles and my wrappers into the trash, then wipe my hands on my jeans and grab a squirt of sanitizer from the wall dispenser.

The pharmacist gives me a sympathetic smile as she quietly names off the prescriptions, one by one, and runs them through the system. I've seen that smile so many times before. They always think they're being kind, but really they're just emphasizing how different I am. It used to sting. Now, it sends a surge of annoyance through me. Despite this, I smile back.

Those are the rules of the game. Keep my mouth shut. Make everyone else feel comfortable. Swallow my pills and stay out of trouble. Don't remind anyone else that there are people like me who live beside them every single day.

Basically, lock up my truth and throw away the key.

She stuffs the heavy bottles into those little paper bags and staples the information packets to the outside, then sticks those bags into a larger plastic one. I hand her my card to pay and drop the pills into my backpack, dutifully thanking her for her assistance.

"Have a great day," she intones automatically.

"Yeah, you too."

Before anyone else can give me the same sympathetic look, I slip out the door, feeling annoyed, yet somehow also hollow and numb.

It's warmer today than it has been this week. I can't see my breath in the air, and the sun is directly overhead. Suffocating humidity forces me to remove my jacket. I can feel the impending rain. The meteorologist predicted more wind and a rise in humidity over the weekend, and my senses tell me she was right.

Popping my headphones back into my ears, I flip through the music on my phone. Drowning out everyone and everything is such an ingrained habit now that I don't even wait for the whispers to start. Settling on a song, I look up and begin to walk, but something out of the corner of my eye makes me stop and stare.

Alexandria Hendricks is walking out of the grocery store with arms full of heavy-looking paper bags.

Alexandria Hendricks, literally the last human being I want to see right now, is walking in my direction, maybe fifty feet away.

Alexandria, the girl who let me die in her basement. The girl who stayed with me when I came back to life. The girl who never suspected that I wasn't okay, that I was locked inside my own mind with no way to escape.

Not her. Anyone but her.

There's nowhere to run, so I duck behind an oversized pickup truck, hoping desperately that she hasn't noticed me, too. Peering around the bed, I see her load the bags into the trunk of a Jeep and close it behind her. Alexandria climbs inside and closes her door. She checks her phone and rolls down the windows, then makes a face of disgust and rolls them back up. Before I have time to question that particular odd behavior, her Jeep backs out of the parking space and pulls out onto the road. She drives right past me, and a horrendous smell trails behind her. I cover my nose until it clears, then watch her turn left at the light and disappear from view.

Relief races through me as I realize that she never even knew I was there.

"Umm, can I help you?" someone calls from behind me.

I startle and jump, turning to see an older man eyeing me suspiciously from a few feet away.

"Oh, uh..." I start, but I'm not sure what to say.

"Is there something wrong with my truck?" he asks.

"No, sorry. I just... it's not important. Have a nice day," I blurt, cheeks burning. I turn on the spot and walk away as quickly as I can.

Yet another embarrassing moment to add to the list. Great. I'm sure someone will tell my parents all about it when they get home.

I chance a sideways glance at the man as I move quickly down the street. He stares at me until I disappear around the same corner Alexandria took less than a minute earlier, half-jogging toward the bus stop in the distance.

The farther I walk, the more that awful smell lingers. It's heavy, like the scent of the alley where I hallucinated that dead dog after work.

Where is it coming from? Was it Alexandria's exhaust? If so, she really, really needs to get her car looked at. A smell like that can't mean anything good.

The bus stop is empty, so I sit in the dirt and leaves and wait. Seriously, I can't wait to be home.

What a day.

OCTOBER 7TH

Dr. Holland wants me to write about my childhood experiences and how that stupid picture I found made me feel. I don't want to do that. Thinking about this stuff makes me so uncomfortable. I don't want to relive those experiences. Why would I? And that picture... the truth is that it made me feel so absolutely hollow inside. Terri-

fied. It's a tangible reminder of how much of my childhood I can't remember, of how much of it I might as well not have lived through at all.

I already know that this whole exercise will be pointless. Every time I try to talk about what little I remember of being a kid, people brush it off. They either tell me it's normal to forget things when you're young or dismiss what I do remember as childhood delusions and trauma responses. Every single time. Not one person has cared enough to actually listen.

I know what they want me to say. They want me to suddenly remember all of the pieces that make up the huge, dark gaps that I have tried so hard to fill. I can't, though. I have tried and tried. I've journaled, done talk therapy, undergone hypnosis... no matter what I do, there's emptiness in my mind. Mom swears that I used to love red velvet cake and that Alexandria and I had the time of our lives at the Township Fair. I don't remember those moments at all. It's like I wasn't even there.

Of course, everyone says that I was there. And now, there's a picture to prove it.

Well, there <u>was</u>. I ripped the stupid thing up. But, it was there.

I hate it. I wish I never found it. I wish I never climbed up into that treehouse in the first place. I had no business being there.

I don't want to do this. The problem is, if I don't write something down, Dr. Holland will know. She always knows, just like she knew that I've been taking the sleeping pills after she suggested I stop. I'd swear that woman was psychic if I didn't know better.

Fine. I'll write something down.

There are only a few things that I really remember. They come and go like flashes of a movie. There's the magic blanket thing. I remember falling off my trike when I was, I think, three? I remember grandpa's funeral. I remember...

The only thing that never goes away is an awareness, kind of.

God, why is this so hard? I'm not sure what I was aware of. Is there even a word for it? My mind? My soul? Religious people say that we all have souls. Maybe that's it. Whatever it was, it was me. It was the things that made me who I was, the stuff that's supposed to be inside of the body and attached to it. But, I wasn't always attached to myself. Even writing this now, I know that makes absolutely no sense.

I always knew I had a body. Sometimes I could even see it and feel it, make it do what I wanted it to do. Those were the good moments. In those small spans of time, whatever I was, the stuff that made me who I was, was actually attached. It filled my head and my chest, my fingers and toes. But, it wasn't always like that.

Most of the time, I was just inside of my body, not really attached to it at all. It was like... like I had been scooped out, I guess? Carved like a pumpkin, but whoever did the carving left all of the stringy stuff in the shell.

Yeah, my body was a shell. That's a good description, I suppose. My body was a shell, and I was in the carved-out space. A lot of the time, I couldn't see anything, feel anything, hear anything, or say anything. It didn't matter how hard I tried.

There was this sick sensation of a squeezing, binding pressure holding me in place, the way my head feels when a migraine starts. My body, the shell, was tight, too constricted. I was too big, crammed inside of a space that was too small, crowded by something that I couldn't understand. There was a horrible, fiery heat. And usually when I could see and hear, I couldn't <u>do</u> anything at all. I heard my own voice talking or saw myself doing things, sometimes very bad things, but I couldn't stop them.

I swear, it wasn't me. There was someone else - something else - in there with me.

Dr. Holland says that it was most likely trauma-related dissociation. I don't agree with that. I dissociate all the time. I don't mean to, but sometimes I check out for a few minutes here and there. The thing that makes this so different is that I know I wasn't alone in my body. That's what no one understands.

I called it possession. She called it Schizophrenia. She won. I was labeled the crazy girl.

She must be right, though. Demons aren't real. They're just stories told in Sunday schools to keep little kids in line.

God, what about Alexandria? What do I remember about her? Nothing really. Not until that day in the basement. There might be some tiny memories with her. Maybe...

I can't tell if it's really her, though. It's just another little girl. I think they're from those moments when I could see and hear but not react. The images are so blurry. Trying to remember them makes me dizzy. After seeing that picture in the treehouse, I'm guessing that it was probably her. That would be logical. I don't know, though. I just don't know.

There's only one clear memory of her, and everyone says it wasn't real. That's why I don't talk about it anymore.

I wish one person would believe me. A single person. Maybe I wouldn't feel so crazy.

There are more of those hazy memories from when I was older. I think they're from when I was nine or ten? It started to get a little easier to break through to the surface and look out into my world. But, even though I remember them, they aren't mine.

Being locked away inside myself with no control was absolute torture. No one has ever understood what it was like. It went on for years and years. How could they understand? It hasn't happened to them.

No one else has ever known what it felt like to internally kick, and punch, and scream, and claw, and cry out to my parents for help without any hope of release.

No one has ever understood what it felt like to look through my own eyes at my family, the family that loved me so much that they would do anything for me, but to know that someone else was moving my body, and saying my words, and kissing my mom good-night, and sneaking out of the house to talk to a strange little boy, and...

No one has ever understood the absolute fear of suddenly feeling the weight of that crushing presence lifted out of my body, only to face down that same, strange little boy with his ruby red eyes and sharp pointed nails in that empty basement.

It's been eighteen years, and the thought of him still makes my blood run cold.

He had this intense, cold stare. Those red eyes raked over my body from head to toe as he stalked toward me slowly, whistling an unsettling tune. It sounded like a nursery rhyme, but it was darker, twisted. I remember backing away, but I tripped over a wrinkle in the rug and fell. My heart raced in my chest.

He flashed me the sharpest smile and laughed at me. He reached out a hand like he was going to help me up, and I took it. I was so naive. I should have screamed. I should have tried to run away.

I didn't know.

The boy yanked me up and threw me back against the concrete wall with some kind of invisible force that sucked the air from my lungs. I tried to scream then, but something smoky and red wrapped itself around my mouth so that I couldn't make a sound, no matter how hard I tried.

I had never seen anyone else move like that. He was fast, and he ran straight at me. I had no time to react. He dug his pointed nails into my chest and stomach, filling me with searing pain, then tugged them down, ripping through my skin and muscles until my body split open. When he withdrew his fingers, they were covered in my blood. He held my eyes with his own as he licked them off, popping his lips and groaning in satisfaction.

I'm sure I was in shock. I'd never felt such agony in my ten years of life.

I tried to call out again and again, but no one could hear me. I was alone with him in the basement. Completely, utterly alone.

I watched helplessly as the boy tilted his head. He drove his fingers into my stomach again with a gleeful giggle, deeper this time, wiggling them. It made a terrible sucking sound. My eyes rolled back into my head.

When I managed to look down, I could see my blood pouring out of me onto the worn carpet below. I struggled to break free from his grasp, but he wasn't finished. The forces holding me to the wall let go without warning, dropping me to the floor, but the boy grabbed on to something deep inside, yanking it out into the open. I had no idea what it was then, but I do now.

He spun me around and kicked me back, holding on to my intestines like a child with a small doll on a string. I twirled across the floor, spurting blood as I spun. When I reached the end of the length, he pulled me back to him, dancing across the puddle-soaked floor with such excitement that I could have sworn he was in the middle of the world's best game.

The boy caught me in his arms and drove inside me again, squeezing and yanking until there were piles of my organs on the floor. I went limp and cold as he dropped me down beside them and crushed them under his crimson-soaked feet. Alexandria appeared on the stairs, pitcher and plate of cookies in hand. She dropped them to the ground and stared, mouth open in awe.

I felt my life slip away as he bent down and whispered into my ear.

"What a lovely little pawn you are, Selena. I shall enjoy moving you across the board to take the unsuspecting queen. It's always the little ones, you know. So innocent. Perfectly ripe for the picking, like fuzzy little peaches in a neatly tended grove. So ready to be consumed. Such thick, juicy agony. So..."

I never heard the rest.

No one else believes me. What kind of demented little kid would make up some sick shit like that?

Apparently, this kind. Everyone thinks that I would.

I would never.

But apparently, I did.

Then, Alexandria was there again, telling me to calm down. She called 9-1-1. She held me while I screamed and rocked. The medics came and took me away.

I can't do this anymore. It hurts too much to think about. I never should have gone up there and found that picture. I won't go back again.

Dr. Holland can shove this little therapeutic exercise. I'm over it.

FRIDAY, OCTOBER 8TH

CHAPTER NINE

EARLY FRIDAY MORNING

Seriously, why do I do this to myself? It's so late. I can't believe I'm still awake.

After digging into my traumatic childhood memories for Dr. Holland, I couldn't take any more stress, so I chose to live vicariously through the problems of fictional people for a little while. I curled up on the couch and sunk myself deep into a new book, intending to read for only an hour or two, but three hours ticked by, then four, and five, and now my eyes are so heavy that keeping them open is a battle, and I'm clearly losing. The words have started to blur together into squiggly gray lines.

Up until this point, I've appreciated the complexity of the story. Telling myself I want to read one more chapter before bed has been a great excuse to avoid the haunting whispers that always assault me as I try to fall asleep. After all, it really is a good book. But it's late, almost midnight. The fear and frustration of the last few days have worn me down, and it seems like I don't have a choice. If I don't go upstairs to my own bed, I might fall asleep right here on the couch. All that will do is give me a serious headache in the morning.

Turning the page, I'm disappointed to see that I've finally reached the end of a very long chapter. So, I begrudgingly give in to the inevitable. I stick my makeshift bookmark, the library receipt, inside. Then, I close the novel and set it down on the little table beside me. It's warm tonight, but cooler air rushes over my legs as I toss the throw blanket aside. It gives me a quick shiver before my muscles force me to stretch. They burn a bit as they expand, but in a satisfying kind of way, like the release that always comes from finally having a chance to stand after being in the car for far too long. I've been sitting here for hours.

My knees pop, twinging for a moment. Nerve pain zings to my feet. I hiss at the unexpected sensation and bend down to rub my legs, soothing away the discomfort. As it starts to ease, a faint sound begins outside my front door.

Slowly, I pull myself up, the pain forgotten. My senses hone in on the noise.

What is that sound? I can't quite place it. *Is something ticking like a clock? No, that's not quite right. It's more like... clicking? Like when someone taps a small metal object against a larger one, ever so gently.*

I take two timid steps forward and round the edge of the couch, silently praying that the floorboards don't creak against my feet. As I draw nearer, the sound changes. The tapping continues, accompanied by something heavier, like knocking, but it's too low down on the door. Even a small child would aim higher than this. *But, it's after midnight. What would a small child be doing outside my door?* If I wasn't so on edge, I'd kick myself for even considering such a ridiculous thing.

I crouch down, turning my ear toward the sound.

Tap. Knock. Tap. Tap. Knock.

Unconsciously, my hand drifts to the door. I splay my palm flat against the surface and wait, hoping it might be the sound of a wayward stick, or some other piece of debris, blown against the door with the force of the increasing wind.

My hand jerks away as a heavier bang assaults the steel. I tip back, clumsily falling onto the floor and catching myself with my elbows as bang after bang echoes through the empty house. Panic courses through me, erasing any lingering desire for sleep. I drag myself away from the entrance and press myself up against the nearest wall, breathing hard.

Bang. Bang. Bang.

I swallow and search my pockets for my phone, but they're empty. I must have left it on the couch. Trying to be as quiet as possible, I half-crawl, half-slide, across the wood floor until I reach the arm and pull myself up, snatching the phone before I drop back down low to the ground.

My heart is racing and my fingers are trembling as I punch in the numbers for 9-1-1. Just as I am about to hit the green call button, the noisy barrage abruptly stops.

I hesitate, forcing my breathing to quiet down as I stare so intently at the door that my vision blurs.

After a few moments pass with no disturbance, I manage to eke out the world's dumbest question, "Who's there?"

No one answers. *Did I really expect them to? Who would outright admit to being there after purposely scaring the daylights out of me? No one. I feel foolish for even asking, and I'm sick of feeling so useless and out of control.* Anger bubbles through me, warming me from head to toe.

"Whoever this is, this isn't funny. Leave me alone!"

Bang!

I jump as the sound comes again, this time much more forceful and followed by the shrill shrieks of something sharp grinding up against the steel of the door. Like nails on a chalkboard, the sound sends shivers down my spine. I'm overcome with churning nausea. Without thinking, I cover my ears and squeeze my eyes shut.

"I mean it! Get out of here!" I yell angrily over the racket. "Get out of here right now, or I'll call the police."

Silence. The awful banging and screeching stop as suddenly as they began.

I force myself up into a crouch to wait and watch, half-expecting some snot-nosed teenager to break out in laughter at the sound of the anger and fear lacing my voice. Or, maybe it would be Nicky. I wouldn't put it past her. She's never tried to hide how she feels about me and has done things to set me off before. I mean, this would be a new low for her, but it's not impossible.

What I'm not expecting is the deafening crunch of a hard, fast impact, so strong that it rattles the door in its frame.

"What the..." I whisper as I stand and back away, squeezing my phone tightly in my grip.

I trail off as the screeching returns, assaulting my ears. I raise my hands to cover them, gripping my phone tighter, desperate to block the offending noise, and stumble away from the couch until I step into the open doorway between the living room and my parents' dark bedroom.

"Who are you?" I demand. I hold on to the doorframe for support, fighting back the urge to drop everything and flee. "Who are you? What do you want?"

Silence falls again.

I wait longer this time, trembling and unable to tear my eyes away from the front door, terrified whoever is outside knows that I'm in here all alone.

Was that the plan? Wait until Selena the Schizo is all by herself to torture her, or worse?

Then, an unwelcome thought surges through me. *Is it even a person at all? I'm so close to the woods here. It could be anything. It could be a huge animal. It sounded big enough to be a bear.*

It feels ridiculous to consider, but it's not out of the question. *What the hell will I do if a bear kicks in my door?*

I retreat into my parents' room and grab my mom's heavy baseball bat. I'd have to be the dumbest person alive to leave myself unarmed against a potential intruder, especially if that intruder happened to be a bloodthirsty wild animal.

As quietly as a mouse, I step toward the window on my tip toes and pull back the edge of the curtain to peek outside. The motion-activated light is on. Someone or something has recently been nearby. But, the surrounding driveway and yard are pitch black. I squint and concentrate, hoping to catch even the smallest glimpse of whatever it was. It doesn't work though. There's nothing to see.

Reassured by the lack of a hungry bear, I let the curtain fall back into place and make my way to the front door.

I hoist the bat high over my shoulder. My hands squeeze the handle, affirming that my grip is solid and I won't drop the bat, before I throw open the door and step outside.

There's absolutely nothing here, at least nothing I can see.

The blackness of the night around my porch is thicker than it should be as it surrounds me. I slowly descend the three concrete steps and scan my yard. The only sounds are the racing beat of my heart, my uneven breaths, and the small rocks scraping beneath my feet. Not even the crickets sing their songs as I scout around the house. It's unnerving. I've never heard the night so quiet before.

"Whoever you are, I know you're out there!" I yell, now thoroughly pissed off. "I swear to God, if you set one foot on my porch again or lay a single finger on my house, you'll regret it. Do you hear me? Get the hell out of here. Leave me alone!"

My voice echoes off the distant trees, but no one else replies. I let out a deep breath, hoping that this whole ordeal is finally through.

A deep, low rumble sounds mere feet behind me.

I whirl, swinging the bat wildly at the source of the noise, but it passes through nothing but air. I swing uselessly again and again until I leave myself breathless and exhausted.

From nowhere, a putrid smell slams into me like a hot gust of wind. I retch and back away, eyes wide with horror. A hulking black shape streaks passed me, visible only out of the corner of my eye.

I bolt toward the house, digging my toes deep with every lunge, and throw open the door, slipping inside and slamming it shut behind me. Twisting the locks, I lean back against the metal and slide to the floor, straining to breathe.

For an hour, I sit there, too afraid to move. There was something out there. It had been so close. It wasn't a bear. I don't think it was a person, either. I keep waiting for the thing to come back, to rip my front door from its hinges, but the screeching and pounding never come again.

When the adrenaline wears off, I work up the nerve to take a picture of the outside of the front door. I shake it as I stand in my tiny bathroom and take my meds, sleeping pills included. I'm not getting any rest without them. No way.

The photo appears in the square. It's completely unremarkable. My door should be scratched and dented from the force of the impacts I know I heard. But, it's exactly the same as it has always been, a perfectly painted dark blue with absolutely no significant signs of wear.

Did I really hallucinate the whole thing?

What a nightmare.

I wish my parents would come home.

CHAPTER TEN

EARLY FRIDAY MORNING

OCTOBER 8TH

Something is seriously wrong. I don't know what to believe anymore. Last week, I was fine. I mean, I heard whispers and had nightmares, but I've dealt with those things ever since I was a little girl.

Why has everything started to fall apart this week? I don't understand. It can't be just because my parents aren't home with me, can it? Am I seriously that weak?

I don't know how much more of this I can take.

I must have hallucinated again tonight. I could have sworn that there was an enormous animal trying to beat down my front door. I watched it rattle in the frame and heard the horrendous banging and scratching. I was terrified. I still am, really.

When it finally stopped and I went outside, I couldn't find the thing. I thought maybe it was a bear or something from the woods. We've never had a bear show up on our porch before, but it wouldn't be unheard of, especially if it was hungry and looking for food. I'm sure it's harder to forage with the seasons changing and all. But, there were no tracks on the ground, and I didn't see any bears.

I must have been nuts to go outside. I mean, who goes looking for something like that? That was dangerous. I should have stayed inside where I was safe. Where was my common sense?

I wish my general lack of sense was my biggest problem. That would make my life a lot easier. It isn't, though.

My biggest problem is these damn hallucinations.

That door should be incredibly damaged after all of the banging and scratching I heard. It should have dents and gouges. But, it doesn't. It looks exactly the same. How can that be possible? It must have been in my head, right? It has to be more hallucinations, doesn't it?

And, I know I saw something run past me when I went outside. Whatever it was, it definitely wasn't a bear. It was way too big and the outline of it was far too jagged around the edges. I've never seen an animal move that fast. After that, I ran straight back inside. I'm not trying to pick a fight with some feral creature.

I will go back outside and check for signs again in the morning. I don't expect to find much, though. I never do.

It's all in my head.

I just want this to stop. I'm so tired of being afraid. Please, someone help me.

Help me.

Help me.

Hel

MY EYES FLY OPEN, dragging me abruptly from a deep, dreamless sleep. I don't remember closing them in the first place. Groggy and disoriented, I reach for my phone and tug it off of the charger.

It's only four a.m. Why am I awake?

After the night I've had, I need much more sleep than this. The sleeping pills were obviously doing their job because I must have fallen asleep with my journal in my lap. A long line of dark ink stems from where I've written my last word to the edge of the page and onto the comforter below.

Damn. I just washed that. I'll have to do it again.

If the pills did their job, why didn't they last as long as they should have? I should still be asleep. Are they losing their effectiveness? I thought Dr. Holland was worried about them affecting me too much?

She's definitely wrong about that. I'll have to talk to her about it at our Monday appointment. Maybe she'll back down on the pills and caffeine thing. *I hope so.*

I push the cap back onto my pen and close the journal, sliding them both into my bedside table drawer. My phone is fully charged now, so I don't bother plugging it in. Instead, I slip it under my pillow for safekeeping and pull the comforter up to my chin.

For a while, I try to go back to sleep, but it evades me. The too-familiar whispers of my name from the dark corners of my room taunt me, and no matter what I do, I can't drown them out. I toss and turn for nearly an hour until I can't take them anymore.

"Would you please just shut up?" I complain. They don't stop. They never do. "You're not even real. Just shut up!"

The woman's overly-sweet laughter joins in with the cacophony of whispers and echoes through my skull.

Why do I torture myself like this?

Thoroughly annoyed at my inability to function as a basic human adult, I head to my closet and pull out clean clothes for the day. The weather app says that it's going to be unseasonably warm again, so I grab a pair of pants and a loose t-shirt, then toss them onto my bed.

My morning shift starts at nine, and since I'm already up, I might as well get a head start on the basics: teeth, shower, shave.

I strip off my pajamas and toss them into the hamper, intending to begin with the shower, but as I turn to walk back toward my bathroom, a movement in the shadows below catches my eye.

Slowly, I cross to the railing and squint down into the living room. A sharp cracking sounds from somewhere in the dark, like a heavy object colliding with glass. The ticking of my grandma's antique clock stills.

"Shit..." I whisper.

If anything happens to that clock while they're gone, my parents will kill me.

Without thinking, I rush down the stairs, taking them two at a time. At the base, I skid to a stop and flick on the light switch, illuminating the large room, then cross the space, stopping in front of the old clock.

The clock's pendulum is still, but the stained glass that adorns it is completely intact. I gingerly pop open the door and set the pendulum back in motion, adjusting the minute hand to match the time.

The sound of cracking glass comes again, this time from the dining room. The mirror... it has to be coming from that giant mirror my mom hung on the outer wall. If that thing breaks, it's going to be a nightmare to clean up. It's almost as big as the dining room table, and it took three grown men to hang it. It's so heavy.

Carefully, I shut the glass door and lock it back in place, then slip around the corner into the dining room. Like the living room, it too is empty. And, like the clock, there are no cracks or chips anywhere to be seen on the surface of the mirror.

That doesn't make any sense. Then again, what does these days?

I inch around the dining room table and stop in front of the mirror. For a second, my reflection startles me. I forgot that I was naked in my rush to save my grandma's clock. Even though there's no one home to see or care, I cover myself with my arms, self-conscious. I feel far too exposed in the still of the early morning.

Though the house is warm, goosebumps rise on my arms and neck. I shiver and try to rub them away, but they stubbornly remain. A chill races down my spine as I turn my eyes back to the ridiculously large mirror. This time, the reflection insists I am not alone. A shadowy figure looms behind me, poking its head around the corner of the living room wall.

Immediately, I turn and stare at the empty space. There's absolutely nothing there. With the lights from both the dining room and the living room illuminating the house, there isn't a single shadow. But, it had definitely been there, just around the bend.

"Jesus, not again..." I groan, rubbing my eyes.

Quickly, I cross the space to the living room and grab my little camera off of the side table. In hopes of catching anything remotely close to what I saw in the mirror only seconds before, I cart it back to the dining room and stand out of the way, keeping my reflection out of the mirror's surface. The last thing I need is for someone to find a picture of my naked body and share it around town.

No, thanks. I'm not interested in that. I'm already a laughing stock.

From the side, I snap the picture and catch the shot that

prints, shaking it as I set the camera down on the table. As I expected, it's a picture of a regular mirror. I toss the picture onto the table, too. My stupid mind is up to its tricks again.

Annoyed, I move to stand in front of the mirror once more, but when I do, a silent scream forms in my throat. My own reflection stares back at me, but there's also the image of an incredibly tall, twisted woman standing only inches away.

She too is naked, and her arms hang limply down at her sides, skin loose and drooping. I gawk at her, but she isn't looking at me. Instead, her eyes are fixed on the floor where a puddle of thick, black liquid has formed. Her straggly long hair obscures her features until she slowly lifts her head and stares straight at the reflection.

The woman's eyes burn a vivid scarlet and flicker as though there are tiny flames captured within. Seeing my terror, her face breaks into a disturbing grin, stretching impossibly from one ear to the other. As it widens, the skin splits, and more black ooze drips down, staining her chin and her breasts. What has to be hundreds of needle-like teeth poke through wrinkled gums, and from behind them, her forked tongue flicks wildly.

I'm paralyzed, unable to so much as breathe, as the woman raises her arms and closes her bony hands around my shoulders. She squeezes them tightly in her grip, digging her fingertips deep into my flesh.

Pain lances through my muscles and joints, forcing my body to react. I tear my eyes away from the reflection and drag them down to my shoulders where crescent-shaped wounds have appeared and begun to bleed. Tiny rivers of crimson race down my arms and chest and onto the floor below.

"Did you miss me, darling?" a soft voice croons. The woman's mouth doesn't move, but I know the voice belongs to her.

The sight of the wounds releases my trapped scream and I tear myself away from the spot. In the reflection, I watch as her fingers slide free of my flesh and her arms drop down to her sides once more. The woman cocks her head, horrifying grin widening even farther on her ghoulish face and eyes following me as I sprint out of the room, too afraid to stop or look back.

I throw open the locks and run out into my yard, all fear of the mysterious animalistic creature from before forgotten, not stopping until I'm almost at the road. Out of air and trembling, I collapse to the dirt, turning back to face the open door to my home. Body-wracking sobs claim me. Hot tears run down my face. I cry until there's nothing left, leaving my eyes swollen and red.

With shaking hands, I trace my shoulder where her fingers had dug in. The skin there is perfectly fine, completely unblemished. There's not even a single drop of blood to show where the wounds had been.

"No. No, no, no," I weep, wrapping my arms around myself and rocking right there in the driveway.

I don't want to go back inside. I don't want to go into that house. But, the sun has started to rise, and I'm completely naked in the yard. The neighbors will see me if I don't. They'll call the police, and the police will call my parents, and my parents will call Dr. Holland, and Dr. Holland will call the psych ward, and they'll cart me away again.

I won't let that happen. I won't go back. I can't.

So, with every ounce of willpower I have, I stand and drag myself across the yard, back into the house of my nightmares.

I tell myself that it's not the house that's the problem. It's me. I'm the problem. And, it doesn't matter where I go. The hallucinations will always follow. They'll never stop, not until I'm dead.

I close the door and lock it behind me, trudging up the stairs to the bathroom and into the shower.

I avoid looking in the mirror. I don't want to see her there.

The mirrors will have to go.

OCTOBER 8TH

I covered up all of the mirrors in the house.

I wish I could throw them away, but I'm sure Mom will be pissed when she comes home if I've dismantled her carefully planned decor. The best I can do for now is drape blankets or towels over them so that I don't have to see that woman again. If you can even call that a woman... I'm not sure.

Whatever it was, it's not welcome here.

I closed all the blinds and curtains, too. Just in case. And, I covered up grandma's old clock.

I can't do anything about some of the other bits of glass and metal around the house. I'll have to avoid looking at them for now.

This is probably the weirdest thing I've ever done. No, I take that back. Running out into the front yard stark naked and having a breakdown at the end of the driveway beats covering up all the mirrors by miles.

I know that the mirrors aren't the problem.

Still, I swear I can hear scratching coming from behind the glass.

CHAPTER ELEVEN

LATE FRIDAY MORNING & FRIDAY AFTERNOON

"Pardon me, miss..."

A light tap on my shoulder startles me. I nearly jump out of my skin. I hadn't heard her approach me with my headphones in.

The poor woman hastily pulls her arm back, clearly worried. "I'm so sorry..." she apologizes, eyes wide.

"No, it's okay. Sorry about that." She hasn't done anything wrong. It's me. I keep waiting for the next hallucination to strike. I'm so on edge, but I don't want to scare her, so I summon up my best customer service persona before asking, "What can I do for you, ma'am?

"Do you think you could help me find this book?"

She holds out her phone and shows me the cover of one of our new releases. I've seen this one before. It's a thriller, perfect for the season. If it's shelved in the right place, it should be on the display near the entrance. I smile reassuringly at her, then lead her down the aisles to the "New Releases" area. We scan the shelves together, sliding books around, but come up with nothing.

"It should be here. I don't think it would have been shelved anywhere else. It's too new to be in the stacks. You could ask Mary at the front desk to look it up in our system for you," I offer. "Our patron computers are down right now, but we're hoping to have them working again soon."

"Sure."

She slips her phone into her pocket and nods politely, thanking me for my time even though I didn't help very much at all. She seems nice, so I smile back and wait until she walks away to turn and head for the most isolated part of the library I can find.

I need to be away from people. It's been a very, very rough morning.

Every unexpected sound scares the hell out of me. I jump at the smallest things. Patrick slammed the microwave door in the break room when he warmed up his coffee earlier, and I squeaked. I literally squeaked. It's pathetic.

My mind keeps wandering back to the ghoulish woman in the mirror. I imagine her awful smile again and reach for my uninjured shoulder. There should be deep punctures from the tips of her bony fingers, but all I touch is unblemished skin. I don't understand why this is happening to me. I don't know how much longer I can take this stress and constant fear.

I hunker down in the stacks and make myself busy. Today's menial task is dusting, which doesn't seem like a big deal to most people, but in a library, it's a colossal undertaking.

I don't mind the work. These books need someone to love them, and I enjoy taking care of them. I pull each of them down individually and gently wipe the covers and edges, then sweep my rag across the shelf before finally returning the books to their places. When I reach one of my favorites, I turn the cover out to face the patrons. It's more likely to be chosen that way, and the idea makes me smile. I focus on keeping that peaceful feeling as I move from one shelf to the next.

After only seven shelves, Nicky's grating voice calls out to me from the end of the aisle.

"Selena, a word, please? Now."

Great. What did I do this time?

Much to Nicky's annoyance, and to be honest, my pleasure, I take my time returning the books that are neatly stacked on the floor beside me. She stares me down as I collect my cleaning supplies, and when I stand to follow her, she marches straight to her office. She pulls open the door, a sour expression still on her face, and motions for me to go inside, then steps in and closes the door behind her.

"Sit," she commands.

"Okay?"

Nicky takes up her customary position of power behind the desk and glares at me. I hate that it makes me feel small. She's only a few years older than I am, but she wields her managerial power over others like a weapon. She's a menace.

I scoot farther back in my chair and wait, fidgeting with the dirty rags balled up in my lap.

"You're scaring the patrons," she announces, voice heavy with disgust. "All day long, I've been getting complaints about your *abnormal* behavior. What do you have to say for yourself?"

Emphasis on *abnormal*. She's been looking for a reason to call me out, and unfortunately, I seem to have given it to her.

"All day long? Nicky, I've only been here for two hours."

She smiles at me with satisfaction. Apparently, this is exactly how she wanted me to respond.

"Yes, but it seems that may have been two hours too many."

Disbelief clouds my senses. *What is wrong with her?* Generally, I try to refrain from letting Nicky know that she's gotten to me, but today, I don't have the energy to do so. I scowl at her and blink rapidly, shaking my head.

"What are you talking about?"

"You need to go home, Selena. For the rest of the day, *at least*."

That is the absolute last thing I want to do right now. The thought of being in my house alone again makes my skin crawl. I know that the house isn't the problem, but the mirrors... Internally, I shudder.

"Why? I haven't done anything wrong."

"You haven't done anything *right*, either. I can't have our patrons upset by your actions. Take the rest of the day. I'll use this time to think about how the schedule for the week will go and give you a call. We may need to re-evaluate your shifts for the time being."

I've had enough. She has chosen the worst possible day to give me a hard time. Before I can stop myself, words I know I shouldn't say flow freely out of me.

"You're sending me home? What? God forbid you take the time to figure out what's going on with your employees instead of instantly judging them. No, 'how are you doing today, Selena?' No, 'what seems to be bothering you?' You couldn't care less."

"That's absurd."

"You treat me like I'm some sort of pariah because I have Schizophrenia. Well, guess what? You're not perfect. No one gave you a hard time when you showed up late to your shift last week. Yeah, we all noticed that you were wearing the same clothes as the night before and reeked of beer. Oh, and that you stayed in your office for the entire day. But hey, Selena has one bad day, and let's give her hell, huh? Let's make it worse. Let's send her home and threaten to suspend her. Let's see what she does then. Figures."

Nicky's eyes light up with rage. I can almost feel it radiating off of her. I don't care. I'm so sick of her and her elitism.

"Get out of my office, now. Go home before you make this any worse with your insubordination. We can discuss your position with this library in a few days when you've pulled yourself back together."

"Yeah, and when I've called my attorney, too." I spit.

This has the desired impact. The color instantly drains from her face.

"An attorney? Selena, that seems hardly necessary given the circumstances…"

"Yes, an attorney. For violating the Americans with Disabilities Act and refusing to support your employees, and for creating a hostile work environment, too."

"I would never…" she starts, but I cut her off.

"You have, every single day that we've worked together. You don't think I hear what you call me? Selena the Schizo. You're not that quiet, and you're not that funny, either."

"Selena…"

"Nicky…"

We stare at each other in silence for a moment, neither of us sure what else to say. I'm not sure there is anything else to say, really. I should have put her in her place a long time ago. I didn't want to lose my job, but she's decided to go out of her way to make me miserable again. This time, it's worth it.

Finally, she sighs. "Go home, Selena. I'll see you Monday afternoon."

I stand and dump the collection of used rags on Nicky's desk, then storm out of her office and slam the door behind me.

I wish people would ask me how they can help instead of immediately placing judgment. I wish they would try to understand. I hate being the loner, the weirdo. I don't want to live the rest of my life like this.

Still fuming over my interaction with Nicky, I step out onto the sidewalk and stare up at the sky. It's warm today, almost seventy degrees, and the sun is directly overhead. I curse my decision to wear pants and pull off my zip-up, tying it tightly around my waist.

Angrily, I kick at the small pile of leaves on the step. I'm not going home. No way. That's just asking for things to get worse. I'll be by myself, left with nothing but my brain for company, and clearly, my brain hates me right now.

That's why I wanted to stay at work. Menial labor to occupy my time kept some of the thoughts away, and if I needed to, I could judge whether I was having a hallucination or not by the reactions of the people around me. I have a feeling that people might freak out if they saw that woman, that thing, show up right in front of them. That would be a pretty good sign.

But no, Nicky had to take the one tiny piece of security I had away. *God, I really hate her.*

Not wanting to attract attention by staying in one place too long, I take off toward the center of town. My headphones pump soothing sounds of running water and crickets into my ears. That was Dr. Holland's great idea. "Play something gentle to calm your nerves when you're upset," she'd said. It's not really working right now. It never has. All it does is make me thirsty.

So, I head for the little coffee shop down the way.

THE CORNER SHOP is bustling with people trying to satisfy their caffeine addiction before the end of their lunch breaks. The cafe is small, so the line stretches out the door. Though it's hot, I slip my zip-up back on and hike the hood up over my head, keeping my eyes on the ground. I don't want people to notice me. It's easier not to interact.

To the baristas' credit, the line moves quickly. I do my best to stay out of the way as customers take their things and scramble out the door. Within ten minutes, I reach the front of the line.

"How can I help you?" He sounds frazzled. I can't blame him, though. It looks like the lunch rush has been chaotic.

"Umm, do you have anything without caffeine?"

The barista gawks at me as though I've just told him that I'm going to rob the place.

"I get caffeine headaches," I add, lying to ease the tension.

"Uh, okay..." he answers, scanning the menu board behind him. "We have some tea, I guess. That's about it, I'm afraid. Most people come here to dial up the jitters, not tame them."

"Sure, tea is fine, " I answer. "Something with milk, please. And a muffin? Whatever you have."

"Tea Latte. Hot or cold?"

"Surprise me?"

"Yeah, no problem. That'll be $5.61."

He takes my debit card and slides it through the machine, then hands it back, assuring me that my food will be right out. A few minutes later, another barista calls my name, and I retrieve my plate and a heavy ceramic mug, then find a seat at a table by the large front window.

People filter in and out as I sip my tea and nibble on the pumpkin muffin, savoring the sweet taste. Sugar has always been my downfall, but Dr. Holland said to cut back on the caffeine, not the treats. I send off a few texts to Mom and Dad.

Mom says that the wedding preparations have been extensive, but they're looking forward to tomorrow.

They want to know how I've been. I consider telling them the truth, that monsters from my worst nightmares are plaguing every move I make, but that seems cruel. From the pictures they've sent and the messages I've read, it's clear that they're having a great time. I can't bring myself to spoil it for them, so I tell them I'm fine and that I have to get back to work. Mom sends her love and I lock my phone, setting it face down on the table.

It will be fine. I can manage until then.

Eventually, the little cafe empties. Only myself, the workers, and a couple sitting near the counter remain.

I lose myself in my thoughts for a while, picturing a normal life. Part of me can imagine exactly what having friends, coffee dates, and vacations might be like. It seems like such a happy existence. But, part of me can't. I've never known that life, never been on a date, never had friends to talk with over a warm drink. I've always longed for those things.

My eyes wander to the street outside, but most people are back to work by now. I've been here for a while. I guess I was dissociating again.

I'm going to have to tell Dr. Holland about the woman in the mirror. That was really screwed up. I don't want to talk about it, though. Why don't I want to tell her? She's supposed to help me with stuff like this. But, what if this is too much? What if this is the thing that sends me back to the psych ward, land of grippy socks and despair? Do I really have to mention it? Yeah, I really should. I might not...

My internal debate wages on until I notice my reflection in the windowpane.

At first, everything appears normal. It takes a second to register that something is off. I don't know why the reflection looks wrong. It's only me staring back, no ghoulish woman grinning from behind.

Then, I focus on my eyes. They're tired. Deep black circles surround them. That's pretty much par for the course. But, they appear a bit sunken in, more so than they should. And my mouth... somehow it's almost... wider? Not by much. The difference is nearly imperceptible. No one else would notice, but then again, they haven't been staring at this face in the mirror for almost thirty years. There's something else... something about the irises. The color isn't quite right. My usual green is murkier, practically brown. The centers are tinted with red.

"That's odd," I whisper to myself. Though instinct tells me to pull away, I lean in closer for a better view.

The camera around my neck thunks as it touches down on the table, reminding me of its presence. Unzipping my jacket, I pick it up, never taking my eyes off of the image in the glass. I lift the camera up and snap a picture. It slides out of the bottom and falls to the table. Without taking my eyes off the echo of my face, I shake the picture until it clears. Finally, I tear my attention away. The picture looks like me, the usual me. Nothing has changed at all.

When I chance a look back at my reflection, it has changed even more. My face is gaunt, thin and pale, bony in places that it shouldn't be, and my expression is stretched too far. I gape in horror as the duplicate moves independently of me, tilting its head from side to side. The mouth begins to move, forming words that I can't hear. Thick, black drool slides down the lips and onto the chin, and the teeth in what should have been my mouth narrow into spikes as the thing speaks soundlessly.

I gasp. The face in the glass is so like hers. *What happened? Where has my face gone?*

My eyes zip around the room. No one is reacting. They're going about their days as usual.

It's a hallucination. It has to be a hallucination. I grip the edge of the table, trying to anchor myself in reality. *I took a picture of my reflection. It was completely normal. What I'm seeing in the glass isn't real. It's not real. I'm in a coffee shop. I'm safe. There are people here. No one else is seeing what I see. I'm safe.*

I breathe out a shaky breath and squint at the thing that used to be me, trying to make out the words forming on its lips. Suddenly, realization strikes. It's saying my name, repeating it over and over again.

Somehow, my face has drifted closer and closer to the window as I have studied the reflection. A cool sensation on the tip of my nose tells me that it's pressed up against the glass. My breath fogs the image before me.

I try to be calm and pull myself away, but the ghastly reflection lunges at me, and even though I know that it can't be real, my muscles react. Survival instinct has me shoving myself up and out of the chair so fast that it topples over behind me.

The room falls completely silent. I know people are staring at me, but I can't see them. The reflection, now banging its forehead on the windowpane, has my complete attention. Spiderwebs of cracks form, threatening to allow the thing to break free.

I can't breathe. Panicking, I pick up my empty ceramic mug and hurl it at the window with as much strength as I possess. "Leave me alone!" I cry as it strikes the glass.

The heavy mug shatters into sharp-edged pieces and clatters to the floor, but the window remains intact.

Before the last shard lands, the hallucination is gone. The window is just a window. The only reflection is my own.

"Ma'am!" one of the baristas yells. "You need to leave, now!"

Her command shocks me out of my stupor, and I turn to stare at her terrified face.

Why did I do that? God, why did I do that?

"I'm so sorry," I mutter as I scoop up my things. "I don't... I'm so sorry."

"Out, now."

"Absolutely. So sorry..."

I dart out of the cafe as fast as my feet can carry me and race down the street, away from the embarrassing scene.

Everyone will know about this. Everyone. I'll never be able to go back there again.

I'm a freak. They'll probably run me out of town.

OCTOBER 8TH

The mirrors are all uncovered.

I don't understand. I know I covered them all before I left for work this morning.

But, they're all uncovered. Every single one.

Even the blinds and curtains are open. This makes absolutely no sense. Not unless someone... or something... has been in my house.

I'm hiding in my bedroom closet. I brought all of my blankets and pillows in here with me. I can't be out there. It's safer in here. No mirrors.

I have my dad's camping lantern for light, and I'm going to try to read to keep myself distracted.

I keep hearing noises from downstairs.

I'm calling Dr. Holland in the morning.

CHAPTER TWELVE

EARLY SATURDAY MORNING

THE SOLID THUNK OF MY JOURNAL ROLLING OFF OF MY LAP WAKES ME. In the darkness of the cramped space, I'm dazed. I don't remember falling asleep, and it takes me a second to register where I am - hiding in my bedroom closet, tucked away from the vast emptiness and horrifying possibilities of the house as a whole.

I can't have been asleep for long. The batteries in my little camping lantern haven't died yet. I've lost my phone somewhere in the mess of blankets, so I feel around for it and lift it up to check the time. 2:11 a.m. The last time I looked, it was a little before one in the morning.

My stomach does a flip as I realize that my parents will be home tomorrow. I won't have to face my fears alone for much longer. Clutching my phone to my chest, I squeeze my eyes tightly closed and imagine seeing their car pull into the driveway. I can almost feel my mom's arms wrap around my body in a warm embrace and my dad's hand ruffling my hair.

I only have to make it through one more day and one more night. Then, this house won't be so empty. Then, maybe the stress-induced hallucinations will go away. Maybe things will go back to normal. Maybe I'll be able to pull myself back together again.

Maybe.

I toss my phone aside and reach for my journal, intending to tuck it underneath my pillow for the rest of the night. It fell face down. The pages are splayed open beneath the leather-bound cover. As I lift it, they flutter closed, but not before a small piece of paper falls out, landing on my lap. I turn the loose bit over and examine it.

It's another page from my journal, torn from the binding and folded clumsily in half. I flatten the little sheet and lift my lantern to look for the date on the top of the page so I can tuck it back into the journal where it belongs, but there's no date to be seen. I always write the date. I frown. It would be very unlike me to leave the top line blank.

My eyes latch onto something impossible as I scan farther down. This is not my handwriting. It's loopy, slanted, neat.

There shouldn't be anything written on any page of this journal by anyone else but me. I've never let anyone else touch it, not even Dr. Holland. Everything inside is very personal, very private. It's a record of my nightmares, my fears, and my darkest thoughts. It's a safe space for me to work out my own problems without other people telling me that I'm mad. There are so many things in here that I've never even brought up in my sessions. I wouldn't allow it to fall into someone else's hands. It stays close to me or locked away at all times.

Yet, there it is, a short entry written by an entirely different hand on paper that clearly came from this book. I swallow hard as I read the message:

What an interesting read, darling. So much anger. So much sadness. So much fear. If I didn't know better myself, I'd say it was a remarkable work of fiction. But, we both know better than that, don't we? We were there. What a glorious time it was, you within my claws, bound up inside of your own body, betrayed by everyone close to you who failed to see the difference.

Poor little Selena. Poor little lamb. So innocent. So small, even now. So afraid. So alone.

I love the scent of your fear. It piques my interest, sharpens my need. You radiate weakness. So ripe for the picking, and you don't even know.

It only makes me want you more. You will see soon enough that I take what I want.

You can't hide from me in the closet, my sweet. I am everywhere you go.

Run. Run as much as you'd like. I will catch you. I will claim you again.

It's only a matter of time.

"What the fuck?" I cry out, throwing the journal. It hits the opposite wall and leaves a considerable dent before landing with a muted thump on the edge of my comforter.

"I didn't write that. I didn't write that. How is that there?"

I shove myself back into the corner, my whole body trembling and eyes wide with terror. Like I used to do in those brief moments of freedom when I was a little girl, I pull my knees up to my chest and rock.

There's not enough room in this closet for more than one person. That's why I hid in here in the first place.

Did someone sneak into my home and find me while I was asleep? Did they steal my journal and write that message just to mess with me? No, they couldn't have. I would have noticed, wouldn't I?

I didn't take the sleeping pills tonight. Even the slightest disturbance would have woken me up without them. That's why I take them. Without them, I would never sleep at all. I didn't want to sleep tonight. I wanted to be vigilant, to stay safe. I'd bet that the only reason I even fell asleep is pure exhaustion from the events of the last few days. So, someone opening up my closet door, taking the journal off of my lap and writing in it, then returning it would have certainly been enough to wake me.

But, what are the other possibilities?

If no one snuck in and stole the journal while I slept, I must have written that entry myself, right? I don't remember doing that. And, why would I write those words? Why would I torture myself like that? Plus, that looks nothing like my own hand-writing.

I couldn't write that neatly if I tried. My own letters are always half-cursive, half-print. I write too quickly to care.

Did I do that? Did I rip out a page of my journal and write that note? Why? Why would I do that? Why?

A horrifying realization grips me, plunging me into a deep, icy cold. The blood drains from my face and hands. I stop rock-ing. My trembling hand rises to my mouth as the truth slips out in little more than a whisper. "I didn't do it. I didn't write that note."

Another thought sickens me to my core.

She was here. The woman from the mirror was here. She wrote it. She's been in here with me, in this tiny closet, my last safe space. She was here. The writing and the message are hers.

My rational mind wars against my instincts, spouting the rhetoric of the doctors and nurses. *That's not possible. How could she have been here? She doesn't exist. She isn't real. She's a figment in my head.*

That's what everyone has always told me, smart, educated

people. Dr. Holland, Dr. Branson, Dr. Llovero, my parents, everyone at the facility...

So why do I feel deep within my bones, why do I know beyond a doubt, that I'm finally seeing the truth?

I shiver and stifle a sob with my fist. *What if they're wrong? What if they've been wrong this entire time?*

I've spent so many years convincing myself that I can't trust my own mind, shoving back the voices that torment me, taking medication after medication, rotting away in a psych facility, being bullied by Nicky and the others, and for what?

I've been lied to for so long.

No. No. No.

I don't want to be right. I want to believe the propaganda: My imagination gets the best of me. The voices and the images aren't real. There are no demons lurking in the shadows or reaching out through the mirrors. No monstrous woman is leaving me threatening messages.

I am safe. I am safe in my own home. I am safe. I am safe.

I am not alone.

SATURDAY, OCTOBER 9TH

CHAPTER THIRTEEN

EARLY SATURDAY MORNING

UNBLINKING, I STARE ACROSS MY HIDING SPACE TO THE PLACE WHERE my journal rests innocently on the edge of my comforter. Resignation creeps in.

I have been right all along.

Acceptance washes over me. Fury burns through my veins.

I'm not Schizophrenic. I don't have an over-imaginative mind. I've been stalked, tormented, and possessed by demons. I've tried to tell everyone so many times. No one could accept my truth. They couldn't get it through their heads, so instead, they left me to fight through all of this alone.

Her sticky sweet laughter echoes through the tiny space, bouncing eerily off of the walls.

"Yes," she whispers. "You've been so very, very alone."

My eyes drift closed and my head hangs down in defeat.

The doctors, my family... They let this happen to me. They betrayed me. And now, I'm probably going to die, alone in my house without ever getting to say goodbye.

"Selena, darling," she whispers.

Her voice is deceptively gentle, but underneath, it's laced with venom. It wraps around me, sucking the air from my lungs. The air in the closet grows thick and warm.

"Open your eyes."

There is a soft tugging on my blankets. I don't want to look. I don't want to see. If I keep my eyes closed, I can almost convince myself that none of this is real.

None of this is real.

The last of the blanket slips away.

It rustles as it slides across the floor. Still, I keep my eyes glued shut. I draw in a deep, steady breath and feel for the lantern. My fingers close around it. Gripping the thing tightly, I lift it into my lap.

Slowly, I raise my head.

I can't avoid the truth forever.

I open my tear-filled eyes.

Crouched in the corner and ready to pounce, her gruesome form stares back at me through vicious, burning eyes. Seeing the fear etched into my features, she smiles. I watch as her split tongue traces her cracked, oozing lips. She digs her pointed nails into the floor, leaving deep gouges behind.

"Selena, my sweet," she croons. "It's been far too long."

If I don't get out of this closet, I'm going to die. It's now or never. I choose now.

As soon as I decide I'm not ready to die, everything happens so quickly that I barely register my own movements. I lunge for the closet door. The knob turns easily in my hand, and the door swings wide. With only my lantern to illuminate the space, I plunge into the pitch-black darkness of my room. I scramble across the floor, slipping on a pair of discarded jeans and falling. I land hard enough that the glass enclosure of the lantern shatters. The impact jars me, sending instant aches through my hands and knees. My only source of light flickers out. I'm surrounded by shadows. They churn and reach, twisted fingers grabbing for my clothes.

I crawl toward the railing of the stairs and whimper as I try to rise to my feet. My knees throb in protest and a sharp pain shoots up my right arm, but I manage to stand. I'm about to descend into the living room below when I make a very stupid mistake. I look back at the closet where I've just been.

It's filled with deep, dark blackness, but her burning, ruby red-eyes peer around the edge of the door frame.

"Where are you running to, my little lamb?" the demon teases. Her voice comes out like a song, split-melodic notes full of temptation. It calls to me, just as the abandoned treehouse had, tugging at something deep inside. Against my will, my eyes roll back into a sleepy haze and I feel my legs begin to give, my body slipping down the railing to the cold floor below.

She inches closer to me, sticky black drool trailing along the floor behind her. The wood sizzles where the liquid makes contact, sending up a noxious scent of burning wood and plastic. I fight the hypnotic urge to stay put, focusing on the grinding, lower tones of the demon's voice. Using the spindles of the railing, I pull myself away, inch by painstaking inch.

"Sweet little lamb, quiet as a mouse, all locked away in this big, empty house. Where will you go when you're all alone? Scream all you want. There's nobody home."

"Stay... away from me... you evil... bitch!" I grunt, reaching the top of the stairs.

That sickeningly sweet laugh sounds, now only inches away.

"There's no one to save you now."

Fingers clawing for purchase on the steps below, I roll onto my stomach and drag myself down. My ribs bounce painfully off of the steps - one, two, three - before a piercing pain shoots through my ankles, followed by a crushing grip, and I'm yanked back to the loft so quickly that there's no time to resist.

My head bounces off of the edge of the top step with a disgusting crack, and a flash of red fills my vision. Instant nausea and dizziness surge through me, but I fight them back. Desperate to hold my ground, I dig my fingernails into the wood. It splinters as she drags me across the floor. My nails split and crack with the force, but I manage to slow my momentum enough to fling out my elbow and catch myself on the foot of the bed. The heavy metal frame shrieks, threatening to slide with me, but standing firm.

Her grip releases and I kick backward, landing a solid blow on the demon's face. All pretenses of sweetness gone, she bellows, growling out her command.

"Come with me, you insolent little brat!"

"Never!"

I kick out again, sending the figure sprawling. As fast as I can manage, I use the bed frame to haul myself up. I fumble with the sheets and run straight into my nightstand before I'm able to orient myself, but before I can take a single step more, the demon is on me again, ramming into me and propelling me back to the railing. I cry out, but the demon only crashes into me again, backing me farther and farther away until I feel the top rail press into my spine.

"Stop!" I urge, pushing back. "Stop! Don't do this!"

A deafening crack rings out as the rail behind me splits. I fall back helplessly, hurtling to the ground below.

My bones rattle with the impact as I slam into the floor. I struggle to breathe, but she leaps down effortlessly, landing on top of me and pinning me down.

"What do you want from me?" I somehow manage to choke out, tasting iron on my tongue. "Please, just leave me alone."

"I will never leave you alone," she snarls, face so close to mine I can feel her hot breath fill my nostrils. "I never have. Everyone else cast you aside, but not me. Don't you remember me, darling? I am you. You are me. We have been Selena for a long, long time."

She brings her twisted face down to my own and licks my chin. I squirm, but her body presses harder into my own. I can't escape. I can't even move.

Helpless, I can do nothing but watch as she lifts one deformed limb high and slams it down into my skull. Indescribable pain radiates through me. I open my mouth to scream, but all that escapes is a weak whimper. My vision fades to nothing. I am lost to the abyss.

CHAPTER FOURTEEN

SATURDAY MORNING

EVERY INCH OF MY BODY THROBS AS I REGAIN CONSCIOUSNESS. I CAN'T remember why I'm in pain. The pulsing behind my eyes won't allow me to focus. Reluctantly, I crack one eye open and take in my surroundings. Sunlight streams into the room through the open front door, blinding me. I groan and try to turn away, but a shooting pain zips through my skull, forcing me to remain still.

Why am I on the living room floor? Why is the door open? Why do I feel like this? I don't understand.

A vicious burst of wind whips through the distant trees, sending leaves rattling across the room. One of them skitters down the length of my arm. I catch it between my fingers. The brittle thing crumbles in my hand.

After a moment, I force myself to rise, moving slowly to accommodate for the soreness. My body screams in protest as I push myself into a sitting position. I must be incredibly bruised, but the pounding in my head is worse. Dragging my fingers through my hair, I feel for lumps or cuts, finding nothing and increasing my bewilderment. Quickly, I scan the rest of my body for signs of injury as well. Nothing there either. No apparent injuries, whatsoever.

I wince but manage to drag myself up to stand, holding onto the back of the couch for support. Another gust of wind assaults me. It's warm today, but I shiver anyway. I grab the heavy throw off the couch and wrap it around me, pulling it tight.

Leaves pile up against the kitchen island. I move to close the door. It thuds as it settles into the frame. What feels like hours passes as I lean up against it, staring at the empty house. During that time, function begins to return to my brain. A series of thoughts form in quick succession.

The front door should have been closed. I know I shut it last night before I went upstairs. I'm not supposed to be in the living room. I was hiding in my closet. There was something... in my journal. The demon. The railing.

A switch flips in my mind, flooding me with memories of last night so fast that my head spins. The message. Her face. Her burning eyes and needle-filled mouth. Being dragged up the stairs. Falling from the loft.

A wave of fear washes over me. *Demons are real. She's real. I've been right all along.* I've never wanted to be wrong so much in my life.

Reluctantly, I raise my eyes up to my loft. I know what I will see before my vision even stills. The railing is perfectly intact. It's like she never even existed. Somehow, she's erased the damage again, just as she has done so many times before. But, I know the truth. I remember what happened. I feel the injuries she's hidden away.

I'm not crazy. There's absolutely nothing wrong with me. No one will ever convince me of that again.

For years, she's been tormenting me. I have no doubt that she's the cause of all of the whispers in the dark, the vivid hallucinations, and that disgusting, rotting dog. It's been her all along. No amount of medication was ever going to save me.

Hatred rages through me, not just for the demon, but for everyone in my life who has refused to acknowledge my truth. For Dr. Holland who used me as a study to bolster her credentials. For Dr. Llovero who talked to me like a child. For Dr. Branson. For my mom and dad.

This last realization hits me like a sucker punch. Without even knowing, I built up so much resentment over the years. I tried so hard to believe their truth. I followed the instructions of so many doctors and drugged myself until I couldn't feel. I let people push me around. I gave up the possibility of an education, a real job, a life full of friends. All of it, every last bit, is because no one would listen, not even my own parents. That is the worst betrayal of all.

An incredible need to break something overcomes my senses. Taking huge, painful steps, I reach over to the little side table by the couch and pick up the remote, hurling it violently into the tv. I swing my arm wide and send the ceramic lamp flying. It lands on the ground and shatters. But, it's not enough. Nothing will ever be enough.

Filled with uncontrollable fury, I ignore my aching body and sprint to retrieve the baseball bat. It's heavy and solid in my hands, and it makes me feel powerful, only urging on my drive for destruction. With resounding thuds, I target and destroy each and every mirror in the house. The silver shards tinkle softly as they fall to the floor.

By the time I'm finished with my rampage, I'm exhausted and out of breath.

My home is in complete chaos. My parents' things... my own...

Heavy guilt settles in, replacing the burning anger until I feel cold and ashamed.

There's no going back from this. This is thousands of dollars worth of destruction. This is shattered trust. Hell, I'll be lucky to have a home left when my parents finally come back.

I sigh. *What have I done?*

I need help, so much help. I don't know where to turn.

Years of grooming and habit have me reaching for my phone. I hate to do it, but there's only one person I can call.

Dr. Holland answers on the first ring before I've even decided what I'm going to say.

"Selena? I wasn't expecting a call from you today. Is everything alright?"

I scoff, falling down onto the soft cushions of the couch and leaning back. "No, not even close."

"I'm so sorry to hear that. What can I do?"

"I need to see you, please. At your office. Can you be available this morning? It's urgent."

"Of course. I can meet you there in thirty minutes. Is that alright?"

"Yeah, sure. Thirty minutes. I'll see you there."

"Before we end this conversation, I have to ask you if you are in danger of harming yourself or others. Are you?"

"No."

"You're certain?"

"I'm in danger, just not from me."

"Selena, I..."

"Meet me there. I'll explain everything."

"Yes, alright. Keep your phone with you in case you need me. I'm on my way."

Click.

I stuff the phone into the pocket of my old sweats. It's hot and humid already today, but I don't care. I'm not changing. I want Dr. Holland to see the truth.

Before I leave the house, I climb the stairs to my loft and grab my journal. I thumb through it in search of the torn page, but of course, I find no evidence that it was ever there to begin with. To be sure, I shake out the blankets, tossing the disappointing things onto my bed when no missing page turns up from within their folds, either.

I hadn't expected anything less. If the railing could be so easily repaired, and if my bruises and injuries could be so readily hidden, a little piece of paper would have been simple enough to magic away.

Hastily, I scribble my own note on the next blank page.

With an irreverent toss, I throw the book onto my bed. Feet stuffed into old sneakers and hands covered in tiny cuts from the shattered mirrors, I leave the house, not bothering to lock the door behind me.

I'm not afraid of anything that would be deterred by a lock. Not anymore.

The things I want to keep away don't care about them at all.

I don't want to hide from them anymore, anyway.

I'm done.

OCTOBER 9TH

If you're reading this, I'm probably dead. It wasn't suicide. I'm not crazy. Demons are after me again.

This woman has been torturing me. I think she's trying to wear me down. I'm not going out without a fight.

I'm so sick of being pushed around and tormented. I'm going to *figure out what this thing is and I'm going to <u>kill</u> it before it can hurt me or anyone else again.*

Demons are real. I'm not crazy. I never was.

Mom and Dad, I love you.

Please, just once, believe me.

I can't do this alone.

CHAPTER FIFTEEN

LATER SATURDAY MORNING

DR. HOLLAND IS ALREADY SEATED AT HER DESK WHEN I WALK INTO her office. When I close the door behind me, she looks up. Her eyes widen as she takes in my appearance and her face instantly falls, nothing but concern written on her features. Without a word, I sit down in my customary position on the couch and grab the sequin pillow. She clears her throat and picks up her notebook and pen, moving to sit across from me.

I don't say anything, so she speaks first.

"Selena, can you please tell me what's going on?"

"That depends. Are you actually going to listen?" My tone is hostile. I didn't intend for my words to come out that way, but I'm angry. She, like so many others, has betrayed me to my core. If I thought I had any other way to make it out of this situation alive, I wouldn't be here at all.

Taking in the anger in my voice, she tenses, almost imperceptibly. "I'm here to listen. That's what I do."

"That's what you're supposed to do. It's not what you really do though, is it?"

"What do you mean?"

"I mean, for years I have been spilling my guts to you right here in this room, and for years, you've been telling me that it's all in my head. You said I was safe. You said demons weren't real. You almost had me brainwashed into believing it, too."

"Oh, Selena…" she begins.

I cut her off without hesitation. "I'm not the one who doesn't know the difference between fantasy and reality, Dr. Holland. You are."

"Is this about your recent hallucinations? I've been looking over my notes…"

"Screw your notes. I'm being stalked and attacked by powerful demonic forces that you couldn't even begin to understand. One threw me over the goddamn loft railing last night. It tried to kill me!"

"I really don't think this is a productive…"

"Demons are trying to kill me, and you're still not listening. You're still not listening to me!"

"I am listening. I promise."

"Then tell me that you believe me. Tell me that someone in this stupid town is actually listening to me. I need help, Dr. Holland. I need help, and no one is helping me. Do you believe me?"

Without even realizing that I've stood up, I find myself pacing back and forth in front of the couch. My steps are pushing thick lines into the shag rug. I'm practically vibrating with fear and fury. I know that I should be calm. I know that berating Dr. Holland isn't going to get me anywhere. Yet, I can't help but say these things. They've been boiling up inside of me for so long, inches away from the surface, burning and churning. I can't hold them back anymore.

When I chance a look in her direction, Dr. Holland has gone noticeably pale. Her pen is suspended motionless above her pad of paper. Her mouth is slightly open in shock.

I stop pacing and stare her down. My eyes lock with hers. I refuse to look away. I'm not going to be ignored anymore. I need her help, and she's going to give it to me. She has to. I don't have any other options.

"Do you believe me?" I whisper.

Dr. Holland shifts uncomfortably in her chair and clears her throat. "Yes, of course. This is obviously affecting you a great deal. I'd be a terrible doctor not to take you seriously. I'm so sorry that you're feeling unheard. Truly."

"Really?"

"Really. I'm going to get you the help that you need."

The effect of her acceptance knocks me back, and I fumble for the security of the couch, utterly breaking down into heaving sobs of relief. Burying my face in the soft side of the sequined pillow, I scream, letting out years and years of heart-rending pain into the soft fabric. I allow myself to be vulnerable, to believe that things will finally be better. To...

I'm so consumed by this moment that I don't even hear Dr. Holland rise from her chair until her voice carries over to me from farther away than it should.

Exhausted from fighting back the emotions for so long, I lift my head from the pillow and wipe away the snot and tears with the sleeve of my hoodie.

She's standing behind her desk, phone in hand.

"Dr. Holland?"

"Yes, this is Dr. Holland... No, I cannot hold. I'm in need of urgent assistance at my office. I have a patient who is experiencing a severe mental health crisis, and I need a team to escort her to a care facility for a seventy-two-hour hold."

My mouth drops open in shock.

"A twenty-eight-year-old female, Schizophrenic with delusions of demonic figures... Yes, I believe medication will be required."

"Dr. Holland... no." I'm once again filled with betrayal... loss... anguish... sorrow.

"Please hurry. I believe that she is a danger to herself and others in her current state."

"I'm telling you the truth. You know I'm telling you the truth!"

"Selena Thomas," she continues on, doing her best to ignore my outburst.

I shove myself to my feet and start to approach her desk, but she only backs away, afraid.

"No," is all I can manage. I can't believe this. I opened up to her, truly opened up, and she turned her back on me. I really am in this alone.

With a look of disgust, I march in the direction of the office door, but Dr. Holland races toward it, too. She throws herself into my path, phone held to her ear with her shoulder and arms spread wide.

"Selena, please. You asked me for help. I'm trying to help you. Go back to the couch. We can talk this through until the team arrives, then they can get you to someplace safe. I'll even go with you."

"Fuck you!" I scream. "I'll never be safe. Never! Not when all I have are people like you." She scrambles to stop me as I reach for the doorknob, but I knock her away with my elbow, throwing open the door. I race through the waiting area and out onto the sidewalk, hearing her heeled footfalls behind me.

"Selena, come back!" she calls, but I refuse to heed her, pounding step after step on the hard concrete away from her office as quickly as I can.

I came here for help, not to be locked away. I won't waste

another second of my life rotting away in that facility. These may be the last hours I have left. I wanted her to believe me. I thought I needed her to believe me. Turns out, there's not one person in this whole damn town I can trust.

Whatever. If it makes them feel better to write me off as crazy, that's on them. I know better. I'm not insane, and I will not go down without a fight.

I'll just have to survive this alone.

CHAPTER SIXTEEN

LATE SATURDAY MORNING

I NEED TO GET AWAY FROM PEOPLE. I DON'T WANT TO SEE THEIR faces. Not one. I'm so sick of the judgment and the pitiful glances. No one in this town has ever taken me seriously. Not when I was brutally murdered by a demon at ten years old and somehow resurrected. Not when the press releases painted me like a hysterical little girl. Not after Dr. Holland published her definitive study of my case. I don't know why I thought today would go any differently. I should have known better. Nothing I say or do is ever going to change that. I'm a pariah. They all think I'm crazy. They think I'm dangerous. They're wrong of course, but perception is a powerful thing. My reputation in this town is sealed.

I'm better off alone.

I keep waiting to hear shouting voices or blaring sirens behind me. I trudge angrily down the main road, but they never come. Everything is painfully normal. People wander in and out of the little shops and talk to each other on the street corners. A few spare a glance in my direction and nod politely. Some of the people I pass stare or murmur something under their breath, but it doesn't matter anymore. I don't acknowledge them. I've never been worth their time before. They're not worth mine.

Turning the corner and heading away from the main road, I come to a decision. If I make it out of this alive, I'm leaving this place. There's nothing here for me. This little town can burn for all I care. It's not my home anymore. Home is a place where you feel safe and accepted. I've never felt that here, not even with my own family.

I love my parents so much that it hurts, and I know that they love me, too. The problem is, they love a version of me that isn't real. They believe, wholeheartedly, that the medical professionals I've seen over the years are right about me. They think there's something wrong with my mind.

I don't know why they wouldn't. I spent my childhood trapped inside my own body, controlled by demonic forces that I couldn't even begin to understand or fight. To them, I wasn't acting strangely. They never had a chance to see me behave like my true self, did they? In those rare moments when I was able to break through to the surface, to escape my bonds, I tried to tell them that something was wrong, but they assumed my stories were the ramblings of a creative child.

I was normal to them, just like any other little girl. I went to school. I played and laughed with my friend. I listened to their bedtime stories and let them tickle me. So, why would they suspect anything was wrong?

But it wasn't me. It was her. I'm sure of it now. She locked me away inside of myself and stole my life.

So, no. My mom and dad may live here, but this place isn't my home. It never was. I've never had a home. That demonic bitch stole it from me.

The bus rushes past me as I turn and trek down the old dirt road. Farther down, I veer onto the path through the woods. I need time to think. At least if I take this route, the chances of accidentally having to interact with anyone on my way home are minimal. I don't want to go back there, but there's nowhere else for me to be. Besides, it's not like I'm safe from her out here. She'll find me no matter where I go. She said as much in her message. She's been doing exactly that for years. I just never knew.

No, I did know. No one else listened to me. They refused to know. They spent all of their time brainwashing me, trying to convince me to fit into their idea of who I should be. And, I honestly started to believe their lies, too. I doubted myself every day for eighteen years. Look where that got me. I fell right into the literal hands of the creature I wanted so desperately to escape.

Screw them. Screw every single one of them.

The intense winds of the last few days have wreaked havoc on the more brittle trees in the forest, leaving scattered debris littered across the road. I nearly trip over a large fallen branch as I stomp down the path. Leaves swish by my legs. I kick the smaller twigs aside.

I'm so lost in the pain of betrayal that it takes me a while to notice that the woods surrounding me are eerily quiet. Aside from the crunching of my footsteps as I pick my way down the empty path, the only sound is the wind whistling through the trees. There are no crickets chirping or birds cawing. The intensity of their absence sets me even more on edge than I already am.

My instincts scream at me, begging me to listen this time.

Something is very wrong.

The path breaks through the trees into a large clearing. In the center, an old, abandoned building looms over the space, casting a long shadow onto the crossroads below. The dirt road leads out in four directions, and in the very center of the crossing is the strangest thing: the remnants of an already burnt black candle. A trail of wax leads away from the stub, then pools around a small divot in the dirt.

Don't go over there. Don't be stupid. Ignore it and go home.

Slowly, I approach the wax and bend down. I run the tip of my finger across the hardened spill. It's cold to the touch. It's been here for a while. I don't understand, though. *Who would burn a candle out here, in the literal middle of nowhere?*

Get out of here, Selena. It's none of your business. You have enough of your own problems to deal with. Walk away.

There's a familiar shape in the center of the hard, black puddle. I turn my foot and place it inside the barren spot. It would fit around my shoe nearly perfectly except that my own foot is maybe one size too large. Someone stood here and watched the candle burn.

Leave. Leave now!

A gust of wind slams into me, throwing me off balance and pushing me slightly forward. I stumble out of the patch of wax and knock over the candle, only to find a recently disturbed patch of dirt. I move the loose bits around with my toe. A corner of what looks like a wooden box pokes through.

Leave it alone!

"Nope. No way," I say, taking a step back, finally listening to my inner voice. "I've had enough of mysterious boxes in the woods, thank you." The last time I opened one, I found that picture of Alexandria and me. I don't know what it is, but I'm not sticking around long enough to find out, either.

Another gust of wind rushes through the place, sending the remains of the building's shattered doors flapping back and forth. It must have been a schoolhouse at one point. That's what it looks like. A very blurry memory of this place takes root in my mind. I've been here before. It was dark. I wasn't alone. There was a boy…

Carter. I've been here before with Carter.

Except, I've never been here before, and I would never have met Carter here. I would never have met Carter anywhere at all.

It was her. She brought me here.

This place is dangerous. I need to go. Now.

As I turn to leave, a deep, rumbling growl sounds from inside the structure.

The smell hits me like a freight train and I gag, inching backward away from the gaping hole where the rest of the doors had been. I can't see anything inside. Heavy thuds assault my ears as though an enormous beast is racing right for me. The awful scent gets stronger by the second, followed by an unmistakable snarl and the click of snapping jaws.

I may not be able to see what it is, but there's something there, and it's moving fast.

I spin and dart across the clearing to the farthest path, the one my gut tells me is going to take me home, ducking back into the woods and leaping over the obstacles in my way.

Whatever's behind me is faster than me. It will be on me in a matter of seconds, and I have no way to stop it. If I can't outrun it, I'll have to fight it off. But, how can I fight off something that I can't see?

The path twists and turns through the woods until I'm almost out of breath. My lungs burn and my thighs shake as the sound of burbling slowly increases in the distance, drowning out the snapping and crashing behind me. I curse the water for being so loud. If I can't hear my invisible pursuer, I'll have no clue where it is. I'll lose any hope of escape.

I reach an old, crumbling bridge that crosses a creek. For just a second, I hesitate. *What if the bridge won't hold my weight?*

I'm dead if I fall into the creek and break a leg. I have absolutely no doubts about that. Then again, I'm dead if I stop running now, too. There's no other option. I have to keep going.

The sound of my name, a strangled whisper, assaults my ears as I leap across the open spaces where boards have fallen into the water below. The creek is higher than it should be, and the remaining boards are slick with water droplets that have splashed up from the rocks below. The bridge shakes and groans, but it stands firm, bearing my weight until I reach the other side and emerge onto the solid ground.

I'm so tired. So tired. But, I don't stop running. I run and run and run until I collapse onto the road, gasping for air.

Only then do I realize the disgusting smell has disappeared and the sounds of the creature have vanished alongside it.

Clutching my side, I drag deep breaths into my lungs. My muscles seize, fighting the very air they need to function. I lay there on the road for a long time, unable to move.

I guess she's not the only one I need to worry about. I should have known that after seeing the beast in the alley. *That has to be what this thing was. It smelled the same. Why couldn't I see it this time? I saw it before...* She has so many tricks. I should have known she wouldn't be working alone.

The disturbance of gravel in the distance finally forces me to my feet. I walk slowly down the road toward my house, keeping to the trees for support. In front of me, a white postal van turns into a driveway and stops in front of a house. A man gets out and heads to the back, opening the doors and retrieving a package, before walking up to the porch.

I know this house.

This is Alexandria's house.

I keep walking as the postal worker knocks on the front door. Sticking to the shadows of the trees, I see Alexandria poke her head through and talk to him, but I can't make out their words.

She reaches out and accepts a package, then closes the door behind her. Before the driver can turn around, I disappear down the road.

I want nothing to do with Alexandria Hendricks. If I never see her again, that will be too soon. I don't know why, but I'm sure she's the reason my whole life has been destroyed. I feel it deep down in my bones, and I'm not going to ignore that feeling anymore.

Alexandria Hendricks is bad news.

I'm not getting involved in that.

OCTOBER 9TH

Dr. Holland betrayed me. Go figure.

I've been researching demons all day and can't find anything on whatever this thing is. Without a name, there's too much information out there. From what I've found, each demon is supposed to be different. They have different motives and different weaknesses.

I've only been able to find general things that supposedly protect humans from demons. Most sites say something about holy water and salt. Some say silver works. Some suggest prayer and fasting.

The problem is, I've never been religious. Sure, I believe in demons, but only because I have first-hand knowledge of their existence.

I highly doubt God is going to save me when I have never given a second thought to going to church. I don't have holy water. I might have enough salt to make a meal.

None of this is helpful.

I need more time.

CHAPTER SEVENTEEN

SOME OF THE PILL BOTTLES ARE ALMOST FULL, BUT SEVERAL OF THEM are nearly empty. So many different medications... The knowledge that I have been putting these into my body for absolutely no reason for so long makes me angry all over again. I should have trusted myself. They should have trusted me. They were adults, many of whom were well-educated, even medically trained. They should have seen the truth. I was only ten. I didn't have their power, their authority. Once they made up their minds about me, I never stood a chance.

Feeling calmer than I've been in a very long time, I pick up the bottles and dump them out, one by one, into the empty toilet bowl. The pills land in the water with a satisfying series of splashes. I don't need them anymore, not now that I know the truth. I never needed them at all. Transfixed, I watch them swirl down the drain when I pull the lever. In only seconds, the entire assortment is gone.

There's a sense of vindication in it. There's also a heaviness, sadness and loss. I'll never get those years back. I'll never repair the relationships that were destroyed. It could have, should have, gone differently. Yet, here I am.

With a sigh, I sit down on the side of the tub and hold my face in my hands. *Something is coming. I can feel it.*

It's after eleven now. The world is well and truly dark. The house is calm and quiet. But, it's too calm, like when everything stills before a heavy storm. I smashed every mirror. I left every single light on. I even sent out a prayer, though to be honest, I'm not sure I know what I'm doing. What I do know is that none of those things will be enough. The darkness is here. I can't escape the ominous sense of dread that nightfall brings.

The woman only comes at night.

From what I can tell, the days are relatively safe as long as I stay in the house. I heard footsteps upstairs when my parents left, but that was only a sound. There are whispers, too. I hear the whispers all the time. But, the ones during the day are always much quieter than the ones that call to me at night. So far, the only significant manifestation I've encountered in the daytime hours is that dreadful dog. It was terrifying, but the beast has never been inside my home. The creatures that come in the night are scarier by far.

There's something about the daytime hours that keeps these things at bay. I don't know what it is. I only know that if I can make it through to the morning, it might buy me the time that I need to learn how to fend them off, to fight back. I just need to make it until sunrise.

I can do this.

I hope I can do this.

I don't know if I can.

My eyes latch on to the heavy baseball bat resting against the tub beside me. The bat goes with me everywhere I go. I don't dare leave it behind. I'm sure it won't kill the demon, but it might buy me time when she comes again. It's all about time. Darkness can only last for so long. Every second counts.

Holding it firmly in my grasp, I cross the bathroom and walk over to my bed where I've left my phone to charge. I send my parents a quick text to let them know that I'm still alive. I haven't heard from them in a while, and I know that they'll appreciate the gesture. Their flight leaves early tomorrow morning, so I'm sure they're already in bed. Still, it seems like the right thing to do.

If I don't make it through the night, I want them to have something from me. I can't hate them for any of this. I'm angry with them. The thought of their betrayal, however unintentional, breaks my heart. Still, I can't hate them. That would make things so much easier, but I can't.

The tv comes to life downstairs as I place the phone back on my nightstand. The sudden burst of sound makes me jump. Aside from my own footsteps and flushing the pills, it's been dead silent in the house. I turned everything off. I even unplugged anything that might make noise - the radio, the alarm clock, the tv - everything except for my phone. So, it should be impossible for the tv to power on. But somehow, that's exactly what it does.

Lifting the bat up to lean on my shoulder, I creep over to the banister and peer down at the space below. The local news anchor sits behind his desk, coffee mug in hand, as he reads from the teleprompter off-screen.

"...now accepting donations of non-perishable items and canned food for the upcoming holiday. Let's turn this over to Bianca for the weather. Bianca?"

"Yes, Dale. It looks like the pattern of unpredictable weather is going to continue for the next few days. Variations in temperatures ranging from highs of more than seventy degrees to lows of less than forty degrees mean that strong winds will continue to rush through the county. Residents are advised to drive safely on the highways and take precautions against these bursts of wind, as some may be strong enough to blow cars into other lanes. Expect downed trees and power outages. I'd recommend digging out those handy winter coats, but don't pack your shorts away just yet. Aside from the wind, we'll have clear skies for the next few days. Enjoy this last bit of sunshine while it lasts. Back to you."

A quiet knocking in the kitchen snags my attention. I blink in confusion as I turn toward the source of the noise. A tall, thin man in a crisp, dark suit moves gracefully along the counter, opening and closing the cabinet doors. Finding what he wants, he retrieves two of my parents' wine glasses and sets them down on the counter with a clink. I watch as he pulls a flask from his breast pocket and pops it open. Thick red liquid spills down into the first glass, then the second. He lifts the first glass to his nose and swirls it, breathing deeply.

"Mmm, such a lovely vintage. Fresh." His voice is discordant, like two notes on different scales have been layered over top of one another.

The man turns and walks to one of the barstools. With a gesture of his hand, it slides out enough for him to sit. As he does, he places one of the glasses on the island before raising his own to his lips and drinking deeply. He pulls a smart, white handkerchief out of his sleeve and elegantly wipes his lips before setting his wine glass down beside the other, then crosses his legs casually, looking for all the world like he belongs here in my house. He leans forward, steepling his fingers beneath his chin and resting it upon them. His demeanor is calm, but there's something hidden just beneath the surface that I can't quite place.

Run. Get out. Get out now. Don't let him see you.

My instincts are practically screaming at me, but I don't

move. I'm mesmerized, watching as he sits there in silence like he's waiting for something.

His gaze flicks over to my grandma's old clock, then back to his glass. He takes another casual sip. Draining his glass, he clears his throat and, despite having made absolutely no noise to attract this unwanted visitor's attention, he pointedly turns his body to face my own.

Seemingly human eyes flash red for a split second. If I didn't know any better, I could have convinced myself that it was the lighting. But, I do know better. Whatever this man is, he isn't human, and he knows I'm here.

"You may as well come down now, Selena. We have so very much to discuss this evening. It would be rude to leave your house guest waiting, wouldn't it?"

I gulp, moving to back away from the top of the stairs.

"Come now. I have little patience to spare. I am very busy, you know. Death and destruction don't happen on their own. Well, most of the time."

As I back into my nightstand and send my lamp clattering to the floor, the stranger lifts his arm in my direction. A thick, red, smoky tendril shoots out and snakes up the stairs. I turn to run for the bathroom, but it latches onto my waist, squeezing tightly and pulling me toward the railing. I struggle to resist. I press my heels firmly against the slick floor and use my free hand to grab onto the banister, but the smoke is stronger than I am. My hand slips off and I topple down, landing hard on my back. Without anything to hold on to, I am dragged down each of the steps. The ridges of the stairs dig into my spine as I unwillingly descend, making me wince in pain with each consecutive bounce.

The man tuts as he watches me, chiding me for my foolish resistance.

"Haven't you any manners at all? Honestly, what are they

teaching you humans these days? It's so very disappointing. You behave like animals. I much prefer a more refined introduction than this."

The strange man gestures again, sliding out a second barstool. As though I weigh nothing more than a feather, the smoke lifts me off of the floor and drops me unceremoniously onto it. The stool wobbles beneath me but remains standing.

"Who are you?" I ask. My traitorous voice shakes, betraying my fear.

With a snap of his fingers, I feel the heavy pressure of invisible bonds wrap themselves around my legs, holding my body in place upon the stool.

"Am I truly so forgettable, Selena? I'm offended. We had so much fun, you and I. Don't you remember how we used to play?"

He tilts his head predatorily in my direction. Bright white teeth flash as he smiles viciously at me. He licks his lips, then winks.

"You won't be needing that," he says. With a wave of his hand, the bat is ripped free from my own. It flies across the living room and hits the door, then clatters to the floor below.

My body feels numb as I watch it roll under the couch. It's completely out of my reach, my only weapon. *What chance do I have of getting out of this now?*

"This will be much more fitting for the occasion. Drink with me. I insist." He slides one of the glasses of red liquid to me. It sloshes over the side and puddles on the island below. "It's fresh. I just procured it from the gentleman down the way. What was his name?"

"S-Stephen?" I stammer.

He tilts his head back as though remembering. "Yes, Stephen. He really was a team player."

"Was?"

"He won't be playing anything anymore."

Blood drains from my face as I understand what he's implying. Stephen is dead. Whoever this man is, he killed him. He's dangerous, and now he's sitting here with me.

"You are being very, *very* rude." He contorts his face into a playful pout. "I offered you a drink. The least you can do is *try* it. Pretty, pretty please?" As though pleading with me, he flutters his eyes. "Try it. I'll be *ever* so offended if you don't."

Trembling, I reach for the wine glass. My grip is weak. I nearly drop it. My fingers feel cold and useless. The man smiles as I bring it to my mouth and take a sip. It's warm, very warm, and thick. It tastes like iron and salt.

Blood. My mouth is full of blood. Stephen's blood. I'm overcome with disgust as the realization hits. Coughing and gagging, I spit out the mouthful, spraying the contents all over the floor.

The stranger smiles and brings his hands back up under his chin. The pose is innocent, but I know he is anything but. He clicks his long, pointed black nails together as he watches me wipe my mouth on my arm.

"I understand. A positive is an acquired taste. Next time, I'll bring O. It's lighter on the palate."

"Who are you?" I ask again. I try to push myself away, but the invisible binding holds me down. I can't gain even an inch of freedom.

The man flourishes his hand at his face as though urging me to look closer. "Come on, you have to guess. It's no fun to give away the game. I know you remember. Put the puzzle pieces together. Try harder."

My mind races as I stare at the man's features. Something about him seems familiar. The shape of his eyes... his pointed chin... a small scar hidden beneath his left eyebrow...

Heat rushes to my cheeks as I finally recognize the man

before me. He's Carter, the little boy the demon used to sneak out to see. He's not a boy anymore. He's a fully grown man. But, there's no mistaking it now. That's exactly who this person is.

"Carter?" I say, shock evident in my tone.

"Not quite, no. Of course, I can understand why you might think so. I did borrow this visage again. It seemed fitting, given the occasion."

"Borrow?"

"Take? Whatever verbiage best suits your understanding. He was mine, and then he wasn't, and now he is mine again. Carter grew up to be quite handsome, didn't he? I find this flesh rather enjoyable myself. It's a shame that it will have to be discarded soon. A face like this is hard to come by. Do you like it, Selena?"

He leans in close to me. I cringe.

"No, apparently not. How marvelous. It thrills me to make your skin crawl."

"What do you want from me?" I scream, trying desperately to break free from the bonds. The stool teeters as I fight, but they hold.

"Me? Oh, no. No, no, no. I don't want anything at all."

I freeze, eyeing him suspiciously.

"Why are you here?"

"Let's just say, I'm doing a favor for a very old friend, one who has quite the vested interest in you. Though honestly, she could do better. Look at those dark circles. Look what you've done to your hands! What a shame."

Her. He's here to help her. I struggle again, overturning the stool and landing hard on the floor below.

Carter retrieves the flask from his pocket and fills his glass a second time, never breaking eye contact with me. Tense silence fills the house as he brings it back to his lips, and with one huge gulp, swallows down the last of the blood, observing me with disdain.

"You really are quite boring, aren't you. Little Selena grew up to be a shell of herself. No life. No friends. Still living at home. But, a shell is all she needs you to be, anyway."

I lash out, kicking at the legs of Carter's stool, but he pushes my feet away easily. Rising from his perch, he bends down, bringing his face close to my own.

"Such a waste of a lovely evening," Carter sings, dragging his pointed nail across my cheek. I feel it slice into my skin. Blood wells to the surface and drips down my face. He grabs my chin and forces me to look up into his eyes. I try to pull away, but his grip is powerful.

"I'm bored. Let's play, shall we? I'll be the cat and you be the mouse. You'll run away, and I'll pounce. That sounds like so much fun, doesn't it?"

Instantly, the bonds around my legs vanish, releasing me from the stool. I push myself away from him as he rakes his eyes over me from head to toe.

I'm nothing more than fresh meat.

I whimper as he slowly creeps closer.

"I'm not supposed to kill you, but I don't see why I couldn't rip you apart and put you back together again. For old-time's sake. That really was quite fun. I could turn you into a ragdoll for a little while. As it turns out, I'm in need of a new toy."

"Fuck you!" I bellow, backing into the couch.

"There's that fighting spirit!" he squeals, clapping his hands together happily. "Now, off you go, little mouse. Scurry, scurry, scurry. The fun is in the chase!"

I pull myself to my feet and dash across the space, slamming into the front door. Carter stalks toward me, shaking his head.

"You don't want to go out there. There are hungry things that wait in the night for delicious little morsels like you."

I twist the knob and yank open the door, only to be assaulted with the same horrendous smell from the alley and the crossroads. This time, I can see the creature before me. It slashes out a tremendously large paw, deeply gouging the door as I hurry to slam it closed.

"You're making this entirely too easy," Carter taunts, moving closer still. "Where is the fun in that?" He glowers at me as though I'm spoiling his very fun game.

I turn to lock the door, trying to keep the beast outside, but it slams into the steel, blowing it off of its hinges and knocking me backward with the weight of the metal. The enormous hound digs its claws into the porch, then bursts into the room.

I have no time to think. I run for the nearest door, slamming it closed behind me. The hound is right on my tail, and I can hear Carter chuckle outside the door. Using every bit of strength I have, I drag my parents' dresser over to block the hound's path.

My breath is ragged. My heart is racing. Adrenaline surges through my limbs. I hurry across the room and throw open my parents' curtains. The only way out of here is through the windows. I have to get them open in time.

Try as I might, the windows won't budge. Something is holding them in place. I check the locks, but it's not that. There should be nothing stopping them from sliding up the track.

"Shit!" I yell, searching for something, anything that I can use to shatter the glass. But, there's nothing. Maybe the bat could have done it, but it's in the living room.

I should have grabbed it again. I should have brought it in here with me.

I don't have time to worry about that. I slam my shoulder

against the panes. I punch and kick the glass until my knuckles throb. Still, the windows remain intact.

I'm trapped in this room. I have nowhere to go, and there are monsters waiting outside.

The same smoky tendril from before slips beneath the door and wraps itself around the dresser. The heavy furniture screeches against the floor as it scoots away.

I have to hide. That's my only chance.

I sprint for the bathroom and lock myself inside.

What am I supposed to do now? I'm seriously screwed. Morning won't be here for hours.

I don't want to die.

SUNDAY, OCTOBER 10TH

CHAPTER EIGHTEEN

EARLY SUNDAY MORNING

THERE IS NOTHING, *ABSOLUTELY NOTHING*, IN THIS BATHROOM THAT will help me fight off a bloodthirsty demon and a seriously powerful demonic dog. I frantically search the room, dumping out the cabinet of soaps and perfumes. But, what could I expect to find in a bathroom? Washcloths, toilet cleaner, shaving cream, hair gel... useless items pile up on the floor around me. I groan and sink down against the edge of the tub.

What am I going to do, fight them off with a toilet brush and a plunger? I'm so screwed.

Outside, the dresser continues its slow path across the hardwood floor. The legs screech as they resist, but they won't hold out forever.

A hysterical laugh escapes me as I have the most ridiculous thought: *Mom and Dad will kill me when they see what's happened to their house.*

But, Mom and Dad aren't the ones I need to worry about.

"Selena... come out, little mouse," Carter calls from outside their bedroom door. The heavy thuds continue. Sounds of cracking wood fill the gaps between his words. "Selena..."

He continues to beckon to me, but I ignore him. My panic is turning to numbness, and that numbness is fading quickly to resentment. I'm really beginning to hate the sound of my own name.

Silence falls as the screeching of the dresser's legs on the hardwood floor abruptly ceases.

I hold my breath and close my eyes, knowing exactly what will come next.

With a final heavy hit, my parents' door breaks away from the frame, slamming hard to the floor. The sheer volume of the impact jars me. Using my feet, I push myself back against the outer wall, listening hard.

"My, what a shame," Carter continues. I hear the door creak under his weight as he steps onto it and enters the bedroom, demon dog at his heels. "How will you ever get out of here? This is quite the predicament you've gotten yourself into, little mouse."

He moves around the room, followed closely by his pet, clacking claws only a beat behind his own footsteps. He doesn't go straight for the bathroom door where I'm hiding. Instead, I hear him open and close the dresser drawers and play with the curtains as though he has all the time in the world. "I'm certain that you didn't think this plan through." He tuts as though expressing disappointment to a small child.

I cast my gaze helplessly down to the floor.

A glint from behind the toilet catches my eye, a single piece of shattered glass about the length of my hand and two inches wide sparkles beneath the LED bathroom light.

Slowly, moving as quietly as I can, I slide across the floor on my stomach to reach for the only potential weapon I have. With two shaking fingers, I pinch the jagged shard and slide it over to myself, gripping it firmly in my hand. At first, I'm afraid it will shatter with even this small amount of force, but it remains intact. The sharp edges dig into my palm, slicing through the skin and causing my blood to drip down onto the white tile floor below.

A shard of glass isn't much, but it's something. I long for a gun, or a knife, or hell, even that bat, but this is what I have. All I can hope for now is a perfectly aimed, well-timed slice before the fragment shatters into metallic dust in my hand. Maybe I can open an artery or stab him through the eye. That would kill a normal person. I have no idea what it will do to a demon. But, it's my best shot. I can only hope I have steady enough aim.

Any second, he and his infernal hound will smash their way through the bathroom door. I'll have no way out, and there's absolutely no chance I could slip by and outrun either of them. It's fight or die.

The sad voice in the back of my head tells me I'll likely do both. *They're going to rip me to shreds.* Carter... not Carter?... He's done it before. I have absolutely no doubt that he's capable of doing it again. And that dog...

I cringe at the thought of feeling its powerful jaws snap my bones and those razor-sharp teeth digging into my flesh.

The footsteps grow closer and closer to the door, stopping just outside the threshold. I watch as he tries to turn the knob, but the lock holds it in place. He raps his knuckles against the pathetic wooden barrier playfully, a series of quiet knocks.

When I say nothing, he snickers. "Is that the best you can do? I'm so disappointed. What a shame. A vanity lock on a bathroom door. Pity. This could have been a very fun game, indeed."

I pick myself up off the floor and raise the puny piece of mirror up in front of me, hand trembling in fear.

What is he waiting for?

Outside, I hear him yawn. "Boring. So very, very boring. Let's wrap this up, little mouse. I'm growing tired of this silly, fruitless chase."

The red smoke leeches in underneath the door, reforming into a thin tendril that wraps around the lock and turns it. The knob twists, and the lock springs free. When the door opens wide, the man is leaning patiently against the frame, inspecting the dirt beneath his pointed nails.

"CeCe," he murmurs, reaching one hand down to pat the head of the hound crouched and ready to spring by his heels. "Go fetch."

A deep growl bursts from the creature's foaming mouth and it pounces, bounding into the small space. I brandish the mirror, slicing each time the dog comes near. Its powerful jaws snap and its teeth grind. I manage to dig the fragment deep into the hound's side, but that only makes the beast angrier. It swats me with its massive paw, missing my stomach by millimeters but leaving long cuts in my shirt.

"Enough," calls a woman's sickly sweet voice.

The man snaps to attention, lifting his body away from the door until standing straight, amusement suddenly gone from his features.

"You know this one belongs to me."

"My apologies, mistress."

The hound lurches for me again, knocking me back into the hard tile surrounding the tub. The tiles crack with the impact and bells ring out inside my head. I lean back for balance, refusing to take my eyes away from the dog.

"Call her off," the woman's voice commands.

"But, we're having ever so much fun."

"Now."

"Yes, yes. Alright." With obvious disappointment, the man snaps his fingers. "Down, CeCe. That's an order."

The hound growls, hateful eyes locked on my own, but it backs away.

Out of breath, I clutch the remnant of glass tighter in my hand, still waving it like a mad woman. Carter smiles at me as though I'm the funniest spectacle he's ever seen.

"What do you want?" I scream.

"Isn't it obvious, little mouse?" he taunts. "She wants you."

The piece of mirror grows unbearably hot in my hand. I hold onto it for as long as I can, but my searing nerves force me to drop it into the tub. It tinkles as it lands. I expect the sliver to shatter, but it doesn't. Instead, a red eye of roiling flame stares back at me from within. It narrows as I hear her sickening laugh fill the small space.

"Did you really think shattering the mirrors would stop me, darling?" She asks. "I thought you knew better than that."

I back away again, pressing myself into the corner of the shower.

"And trying to kill a demon with a simple piece of glass? Selena, my sweet. That was very foolish indeed."

"Leave me alone," I plead. "I'll do anything you want. Just leave me alone."

"Aw, but you'll do anything that I want regardless. That's how this works. I slip inside, and you disappear. It's so easy, truly. We've done this before, many, many times."

"No. No!"

"No?"

"No. I won't be your plaything anymore. This is over. No more."

She laughs and Carter joins in. The discordant sounds make my head spin. I clench my hands into fists, focusing on the painful cuts from the mirror to keep myself in the moment.

"That's not how this works, dear. You have no choice. You're mine, and you always have been."

"You're mine." She says it like I'm nothing, a thing to be played with and discarded at her will. Those simple words fill me with white-hot rage as she laughs again.

Not anymore. I won't let this go on any longer. I'd rather die than be trapped inside.

She watches me closely as I bend down to pick up the shard of glass. Her eye tilts as though she has cocked her head. I turn the tiny mirror over in my hand, angling the reflection away from me.

Carter watches me with faint amusement as I bring the sharp edge of the glass to my forearm. Crying out in pain, I pierce the pointed tip into my flesh and drag it up, leaving a deep, gushing wound from my wrist to my inner elbow. I repeat this on the other arm, then drop the shard to the porcelain.

"I'll give her some credit," Carter says, one eyebrow raised. "At least this one has spunk. What an interesting move to make." He pops his lips and shakes his head as he moves closer.

I watch him with heavy eyes, feeling my muscles relax as I drop down to the slippery surface below. Warm puddles of crimson form beneath the jagged gashes in my arms. Cold seeps in. I feel myself slipping away.

The sensation doesn't last long.

Horror consumes me as the puddles retract, blood disappearing back into my veins.

"No... No!"

"Oh, yes," she whispers.

The muscles stitch back together as the last drops disappear, then the skin reforms where the gashes had been only seconds before. No evidence of the injuries remains.

I grab the shard and slash at myself again and again, but

this time, no cuts form. The man reaches down and plucks my salvation from my hand, grinding it to dust in his own.

"She's ready," he says, seating himself on the edge of the tub.

"I know. She's been ready for a while now."

"By all means, mistress, claim your prize."

Searing pain lances through me, filling my body from head to toe. I spasm, foaming at the mouth as I feel her essence of blistering flame slip inside.

It's so tight. It's so tight in my skin. There's no room. My skin stretches and splits. But it doesn't. It looks exactly the same. The feeling of being ripped away from my body returns. I haven't felt this sensation in years. Whatever it is that makes me who I am is stripped away, bound and squeezed, plunged deep below the surface. *So tight. Too tight.* I squirm and struggle to break free. I kick. I punch. I scream. I can't breathe. I can't think. I can't move. I can't...

The world falls out from under me and I drop into an endless black void.

She laughs.

I am nothing.

I'm bound inside once more.

CHAPTER NINETEEN

EARLY SUNDAY MORNING

"That was certainly a spectacular show. I haven't seen torture that exquisite in a long time," the man says as he refills one of the wine glasses.

"That is because you are slipping, darling," I hear myself answer. The sound of my voice bounces around inside my head. It's mine. I know it's mine. But it's not mine, either. It's hers.

It's ours, I hear her think. A discordant, tinkling laughter follows, a wind chime in the middle of a fervent storm.

I watch as my own hand reaches out to accept the glass, a glass I would never take. She swirls it like fine wine.

"Slipping? I'm insulted. I would never..."

"Iroth, you know that's not true. When was the last time you disemboweled someone? That has always been your favorite pastime. I doubt even the poor dear you've bottled for the evening suffered much damage. Come now. Be honest with yourself."

Iroth? Is that his name?

He tips his head back in derision. "Do not imply that I am weak. I am not."

"Of course not. I'm quite aware of your capabilities. What I want to know is why you have suddenly become so... well, simple."

"Simple?" Iroth makes no attempt to hide the thinly veiled contempt in his statement. "Now you insult me on purpose."

"And how did you come about this vintage in my glass?" she taunts. My voice becomes sticky sweet, burnt sugar.

I would never speak like that. What am I? A Southern belle?

Iroth refills his own glass and takes a shallow sip. "I slit his throat from ear to ear and fed his heart to my dog. She deserved a little treat. I had to recall her last night before she could finish Alexandria. It left her... mopey."

"See, simple." I watch in horror as she sips on the salty liquid, too. The taste of it fills my senses. I feel it slide down my throat and settle in my stomach, thick and warm. "Days past, you would have disassembled the boy, one piece at a time. You did it to this one, didn't you? Slitting his throat... Whatever has become of you, old friend?"

He chuckles, reaching down to stroke the jagged spikes along the hound's back. It nuzzles into his leg fondly, and when he stops, it huffs. "Honestly, I nearly decapitated the thing. I did it with my own hands. What more could you want from me? I'm distracted. I have other priorities at the moment."

"Yes, the ring. You should never have lost it to begin with."

"I know."

She leans back against the arm of the couch and sighs. One of my legs crosses over the other, and she smoothes out the fabric of my pajamas, picking at an errant fuzz on the knee. "How much time do you have?"

"Not long."

"And what will you do if she doesn't find and return your ring? What then?"

"She'll find it. From what I can tell, she's inherited her grandmother's intelligence, though not her backbone, admittedly. Nor her mother's, either. This one is so... sheltered. I was expecting more of a fight."

"Do not underestimate the Hendricks child. You know the depth of her family's magick as well as I."

"She's a fragile little thing," he spits. "We should have left her for the wraiths."

"She may not be as fragile as she looks."

"I am not an imbecile."

"I never said you were." She tips the contents of the glass into my mouth once more, licking the drops from my lips after she swallows. "What you are is cocky, impulsive. It will be the end of you one day."

"Perhaps you're right. But the game will be fun until the very last."

She laughs and reaches out to squeeze his free hand.

He strokes the back of my hand with his thumb.

"You must see this through, Iroth. No matter the cost. The Hendricks family cannot retain possession of the ring. The knowledge they could gain..."

"Yes, yes. I know. I'll see it done."

"See that you do. As long as the witch has it, we are all vulnerable."

"I will not fail you again."

My grandma's clock chimes loudly five times. The hound rises beside Iroth and growls, then stalks pointedly toward the door.

"Nearly sunrise."

"So it is."

Iroth stands, making a show of stretching his long arms and legs. He straightens his suit and snaps his fingers. With a whoosh of red smoke, a fedora appears in his hands. He spins and bows to her - to me - and dons the hat with a flamboyant wave.

"Scurry along, Iroth. You have much to attend to."

"Mistress." He turns to leave, following the hound out the door.

Before he takes his last step through the now gaping frame, I hear myself call out. "Don't be a fool. We need her. This may all be a game to you, but losing comes with a heavy price. You have been warned."

He chuckles and shakes his head but says no more. She watches as he disappears into the faint morning light.

Sleep, I hear her inner voice command.

And I do.

SOMETIME LATER

CHAPTER TWENTY

SOMETIME LATER

I HAVE NO IDEA HOW LONG SHE'S KEPT ME UNDER THIS TIME. WHILE she's in complete control of my body, it's like I cease to exist. There is no sensation apart from those of the torturous squeezing, of being bound inside and shoved far, far down, and the unbearable scorching of being consumed by fire. I can scream, and squirm, and kick, and tear at the empty blackness that surrounds me. It gets me nowhere at all.

So, when some small part of my consciousness returns, I know that she has allowed it. For whatever reason, she wants me to see what's happening. I'm not sure I want to. I know what demons like her, like her *'friend'* Iroth, are capable of.

I'm startled out of my isolation by the motion of a swing moving beneath me. The chains binding it to the covered porch creak as it rocks back and forth. It's dark, clearly late at night, and the air has grown cold, much colder than it had been the night she overcame me. I feel my face twist into a smile before I hear my own voice say words that I do not wish to speak.

"What a beautiful night," she says. I can't see who she's talking to. She won't let me turn my head.

Someone beside me jumps up and out of the swing, turning to look at me - at us - in bewilderment.

"Selena?" she asks, thoroughly shocked and confused.

"Selena?" I hear myself answer. There's a hint of feigned confusion in my voice as if she has no idea what this other woman is talking about.

She's talking about me. You know that! Get out of me. Get out of me right now!

Hush, darling. You're simply wasting your time.

A shadow covers most of the other woman's face. I can only make out her mouth. It's full and rather round, attractive.

I should know her. Why can't I think of her name?

"Yes," she says. I can hear the disbelief in her tone. "When did you get here? How did you get here?"

"Right," she replies. It's all an act, fake recognition as though she hasn't known who the other woman was talking about all along. "That's what I called myself before."

"Before?"

"Yes, before. Back when I sent Iroth here to do my bidding." She chuckles softly, a laugh that could never be my own. "Forgive my memory. I've been busy since we last spoke."

The other woman's mouth falls open in horror as she takes a tentative step backward, but my hand lazily reaches out to pat the seat beside me. Compelled by the demon's magic, I watch as her legs move forward of their own accord. I know that struggle, the feeling of being overcome by something far more powerful than anyone could hope to comprehend, the futility of resisting.

As she drifts closer, her face emerges from the shadows into a solid beam of moonlight. She stares at me, and horror sinks into my stomach as I realize who she is. Alexandria Hendricks, my supposed childhood friend.

"I've shown you a courtesy by giving you time to grieve your loss," my stolen voice says. She reaches out with my hand and takes Alexandria's into her own. A band of silver around her thumb glints in the moonlight. My own thumb strokes hers almost lovingly where the ring seems to be fused to her skin. The sensation of it makes me queasy.

My stolen voice speaks again. "But, the time for leniency is through. You have not held up your end of the deal, Alexandria. The favor was given, but the price was not paid."

"Deal? Price?" she blurts.

Leave her alone, I implore.

The demon says nothing this time, ignoring me completely.

"The terms of the contract you struck with my poor, deceased Iroth were very clear. You owed him a favor, completed to his satisfaction, or you owed him a soul to do with as he pleased. As Iroth is no more, it stands to reason that you did not uphold your part of the agreement."

"How do you know about this?" she asks. Discomfort is etched into her features.

I feel her try to tug her hand away, but the demon grips it tightly in my own. Alexandria's bones shift and her tendons squish under the intensity of the squeeze.

"How do I know? Why, because I wrote the contract, silly thing!" she answers gleefully. "Did you truly think that Iroth was the only demon to whom you are beholden? Iroth may have held the contract while he was still alive, but his essence belonged to me. Therefore, any deal you struck with my demon is a deal struck with myself, and I am not one to allow a binding agreement to be cast aside."

"No, that doesn't make sense. You were a little girl, like me."

"And Iroth was a little boy," the demon says. She imitates empathy, an emotion I know she could never feel. "What difference does that make, Alex? A body is only a physical embodiment of the essence. You know that."

"But, you were my friend. We grew up together. You lived just down the road from me for years! We played in the woods and pretended to be teachers in the schoolhouse. You're not saying that…"

"Yes, yes. That's all true enough, I suppose. The form I borrowed did age alongside you, and we did play together for a time. It was a very long game for me. I'm glad it's finally coming to an end."

Form? I scream. *You're talking about me. I am not an object to be played with.*

Oh, but you are. You're mine.

I recoil at the demon's acknowledgment. The intense binding sensation constricts even tighter as though she is trying to make a point.

She's right. I'm helpless. I'm nothing. I'm lost.

"No," Alexandria chokes out. Her eyes are wide with horror.

A sharp stab of pity shears through me. I can't help her. I want to help her so badly. I'm willing every ounce of my consciousness to seep out, to regain control of even one finger.

But, nothing happens.

"Yes," my voice answers. I feel my own smile twist into a hateful smirk.

"But, Iroth is gone. The contract is void," Alexandria stammers, pleading with the demon inside me. "It's over."

"True, in some ways you have won. You have forced my hand, so here I am, appearing before you in person, forced to once again inhabit this pitiful excuse for a mortal so that I may claim my payment."

I am not pitiful! I am only what I am because of everything you stole from me! You stole my life. You stole my body.

I will take much more than that from you before the end.

"But, the payment remains mine to claim. After all these years and all of that careful training Elizabeth gave you, you still failed to heed your grandmother's warning, Alexandria. Magick always comes with a price."

"I paid the price. I paid it with my grandmother's life!" Alexandria shouts. She tries to stand, but my free hand reaches out and pins her legs down with ease.

"Her life was not yours to claim. And Iroth's essence was not yours to destroy. There are rules, Alexandria. I will not allow them to be broken."

In a swift movement, my hands rise and pick up Alexandria's, the one wearing the silver ring. The demon holds it between both of my own, squeezing so tightly that I'm certain Alexandria's bones will break within my grip. I feel myself smile and tilt my head menacingly. My vision flashes ruby red.

"I don't want to die," the other woman whispers, voice full of fear.

Aw, doesn't she sound so much like you? It's adorable, really.

Leave her alone! Leave her alone, damn it!

"Oh, you're not going to die. In fact, you're going to live for a very long time."

Heat surges through my hands and Alexandria's face grows pale with pain. I watch as she struggles to breathe, lifting her head up as though she can clear her airway with the motion. She spasms and chokes, trying to pull away, but it's no use.

"Iroth's deal never specified what kind of torture you would be forced to endure should you fail to meet his demands, and I've thought of just the thing."

What are you doing to her? Stop it. Stop it!

Just you wait and see, sweet Selena. It's delicious. It's going to be such fun.

"What better way could there be to torture you, a devoted witch who wanted nothing more than to avenge the deaths of her mother, and now her grandmother, than to turn you into the creature you hated most."

"No!" she gasps.

No, I echo. *Let her go. Let her go!*

"Oh, yes," my voice croons. "Yes, it's just the thing. You will take Iroth's place at the crossroads for eternity. One essence for another."

Alex's eyes widen. Her irises expand, filling the whites of her eyes with a deep, dark black. She stiffens, growing eerily still.

"Rest now, Alexandria," my voice commands. "We have many millennia together, you and I. You'll need your strength to claim my souls. As above, so below, like you witches always say. The circle is sealed."

Alexandria's body collapses back into the swing, seemingly lifeless. Uncontrollable manic laughter escapes from my lips, and whatever non-corporeal form I have cowers back into the dark.

What have you done?

Exactly what I came here to do, Selena.

You're an evil, heartless bitch.

More discordant, tinkling laughter rings through my mind.

Mmm, yes. Say that again, darling. I like it.

The demon reaches into my jacket pocket and pulls out a small silver mirror and a tube of bright red lipstick. She opens the compact and pops the lid off of the tube, raising the mirror to my face and smearing the vibrant color across my lips.

I look nothing like myself. Nothing at all.

In the time that I have been bound, she's changed so much. My right nostril is pierced. My once longer hair has been shorn to a chin-length bob and straightened. My eyes are lined with thick black liner and covered in dark shadow.

I don't even recognize myself anymore.

That's because this body doesn't belong to you. This body is mine. It will never be yours again.

I scream and rail against my bonds, but she only laughs.

"Oh, Selena! Isn't it simply wonderful to be among friends?" I hear myself say. She stands and returns the mirror and lipstick to my coat pocket, then easily lifts Alexandria from the swing and drapes her over my shoulder. "Don't worry, my dear. I'll make your containment interesting. I have so many plans."

Get out of my body! Get out of me right now!

"Don't be a nuisance. I grow tired of your rebellion."

Get out of me! Get out! Get out!

I feel myself sigh as though irritated. "That will be enough for tonight," she commands. "Back down you go."

A sickening sensation of falling sends my consciousness down, down, down.

I cease to exist once more, consumed by the burning void.

EPILOGUE

LOCAL COLLEGE STUDENT MURDERED IN OWN HOME

Sources report that twenty-two-year-old Stephen Bennett was found murdered in his family home only hours ago. Stephen's mother, Stacy Bennett, discovered his body in his room when she went to check on him after he did not come down for breakfast. Investigators are still stationed outside of the family's home at this time.

The deceased was home from college this term due to difficulties that resulted in being placed on academic probation. It is unclear what these difficulties may have been, as the university refuses to divulge this information due to FERPA legislation.

Police have not yet released many details regarding Stephen's death, only that the matter is being investigated as a homicide. Authorities urge citizens to remain calm, stating that although tragic, they believe this to be an isolated incident. We have reached out for further information and have been assured that it will be provided as new details arise.

Stacy Bennett is not available for comment.

If you have any information that may be useful in the investigation of Stephen Bennett's death, please call the local hotline at 555-637-9672.

TWO FOUND DEAD IN FAMILY HOME

Two local residents, Frank Thomas (57) and Judy Thomas (52), were found deceased in their homes late Wednesday afternoon. Howard Zimmerman, the general manager of Pritchett Financial, became suspicious of Mr. Thomas's extended absence following a planned vacation from which he was meant to return on Sunday, October 10th. Mr. Thomas, who rarely missed a day of work, never made it back to the office. At around 3 pm yesterday, October 12th, Mr. Zimmerman made a personal visit to the family's home and was horrified by what he found.

"I've never seen anything like it," Mr. Zimmerman told the police. "When I went to knock on the front door, it swung open. I called out to Frank, but no one answered. It sounded like the tv was on inside, so I thought they might not have heard me. That's when I decided to go in. I knew something was horribly wrong when I noticed the smell..."

Mr. Zimmerman went on to say the following:

"I found Judy first. God, that poor woman. Her body was in pieces. I could see that someone had tied her up to the dining room table because there were still ropes around her ankles and wrists, but her arms and legs... Well, they weren't attached to her body anymore. I vomited right there on the dining room floor.

"Frank was upstairs in the loft. He had been ripped open from collarbone to waist and his intestines... someone used them to hang him from the ceiling fan. It was still spinning. There was so much blood. I'll never be able to forget what I saw."

As of last night, the police department has publicly stated that they will be pursuing this as a homicide investigation.

"Though there were no signs of forced entry, it is very clear that these injuries could not have been self-inflicted. We are examining evidence collected from the scene as quickly as we can. So far, all fingerprints and DNA collected at the scene belongs to those who reside in the family home."

Selena Thomas (28), daughter of Frank and Judy Thomas, was not available for comment. Selena Thomas suffers from severe Schizophrenia seemingly stemming from an alleged incident that occurred at the residence of recently deceased Elizabeth Hendrick's home when she was only ten years old. She spent many years in an inpatient psychiatric care facility but was released from the facility at the age of eighteen. Sources claim that although Selena does not typically demonstrate any violent tendencies, her behaviors as of late have been strange.

"You should have seen her at the coffee shop the other day," one resident stated. "She looked wild. She just started talking to herself and then freaked out and threw a whole mug at the window. I'm surprised it didn't shatter. The barista kicked her out after that."

Another resident had the following to say:

> "Is she the blonde girl who works at the library? Yeah, she ran into me the other day. She was very disturbed, screaming about some scary-looking dog. I didn't see anything, and I told her that. That seemed to make her angry. She disappeared pretty quickly after that."

At this time, there are no standing accusations against Selena Thomas in regard to the deaths of her parents. However, it appears that no one has seen or heard from her since Saturday morning.

Police have not yet stated whether they believe this incident is connected to the recent murder of Stephen Bennett, neighbor to the Thomas family.

If you have any information regarding the deaths of Frank and Judy Thomas, the death of Stephen Bennett, or the whereabouts of their daughter, please call the local hotline at 555-637-9672.

MISSING PERSONS

IN YET ANOTHER disturbing turn of events, Alexandria Hendricks (27), daughter of the late Corinne Hendricks and granddaughter of the late Elizabeth Hendricks, has now been reported missing to local authorities.

Jameson Nichols, the mail carrier assigned to Pinecrest Drive, reported Ms. Hendricks missing after more than a week of attempted mail deliveries resulted in a large pile on the porch that seemed out of character for the young woman.

"I have always had a bit of a crush on Alexandria," Jameson told our reporters. "I made it a point to knock on her door and try to deliver her mail personally, you know? I don't think she returned my feelings, but she didn't seem to mind. She's always been very kind. Her grandma was the same way before she passed, rest her soul."

Police investigated the home and found the back door to the house open. There appeared to be no other disturbances inside the home. However, upon further investigation, they found the desiccated bodies of many of Ms. Hendrick's chickens inside a substantially damaged chicken coop on the premises. Ms. Hendrick's wallet and keys were found in the home, and her car was still in the driveway.

Alexandria Hendricks is not the first person to go missing in our town in these last few weeks. Police are still searching for Selena Thomas (28) who has now officially been designated as a missing person, as well as a person of interest, after the death of her parents, Frank Thomas (57) and Judy Thomas (52) only two weeks prior.

If you have any information regarding the disappearances of Alexandria Hendricks or Selena Thomas, please call the local hotline at 555-637-9672.

THANK YOU FOR READING!

Thank you for reading *Bound and Betrayed,* book two of Cursed Souls. I hope you have enjoyed this work.

Do you have questions for the author? If so, reach out to me at smoran@obsidianinkwell.com and you might have them answered!

Please feel free to leave an honest review on Amazon or Goodreads. I look forward to writing for you again soon!

Want more from Samantha Moran? Don't forget to sign up for her newsletter at samanthamoran.nct!

Keep reading for an excerpt from Samantha Moran's award-winning novel, *The Ruin,* and be sure to check out her list of published works!

QUESTIONS FOR THE AUTHOR

Q) How do you feel about people who have been diagnosed with Schizophrenia?

One thing I want to make very clear is that I harbor no ill-will or negativity toward anyone diagnosed with mental health conditions. I understand that mental health conditions are widely present in society and caused by many different circumstances, some of which remain unknown. According to the World Health Organization, Schizophrenia affects as many as one in three hundred people worldwide (WHO). Many people who live with Schizophrenia can live relatively normal lives with the assistance of medications, therapies, support systems, and other medically-based treatments coordinated with their doctors.

All that is to say that any negativity in this text regarding people who live with Schizophrenia is intended to be commentary on how society as a whole treats those who are labeled as "different" and how such treatment impacts those who are viewed in such a manner. The attitudes of characters present within this text do not reflect my own beliefs.[1]

. . .

Q) Why did you choose to continue the series by talking about Selena's human experiences?

When I decided to write *Bound and Betrayed,* I tossed around several ideas for how to continue the series. One thing that stuck out to me was that my readers really enjoyed the twist ending of *Dealings in the Dark.* So, I thought it would be fun to explore Selena's experience and fill in some of the gaps between what happened to her in her childhood and how she came to be possessed by a demon once more.

As with Iroth, the demon that possesses Selena needs to have a physical form. Iroth chose to possess a little boy when Alex and Selena were young in order to gain Alex's trust. In *Dealings in the Dark,* it is revealed that he later possesses the same little boy, who has now grown up, when he comes to interact with Alex again.

It felt right for a similar process to take place for Selena. She was possessed frequently as a child, then the female demon came back to claim her once more. It creates a sense of symmetry.

Q) Why did you choose to focus on the diagnosis of Schizophrenia for Selena?

When I was constructing Selena's narrative, her experiences, symptoms as her doctors would have called them, felt most strongly aligned with those of Schizophrenia. According to the Mayo Clinic, people who experience Schizophrenia typically have some or all of the following symptoms: delusions, hallucinations, disorganized speech, disorganized or abnormal behavior, and difficulty functioning in day to day life (Mayo Clinic).

As a child, Selena told the police and many medical professionals that she had been possessed by a demon, murdered, and brought back to life. In my mind, this would have been classified as a delusion because it would have seemed unbelievable to those who have not experienced it. Selena also hears things and sees things that others cannot, and therefore these would be misconstrued as hallucinations. Additionally, Selena engaged in behaviors that others would likely consider abnormal, such as throwing the coffee cup in the cafe or covering and smashing all of the mirrors in her home. Finally, it is apparent that Selena experiences social withdrawal, as she has limited interactions with those outside of her family and therapist. Therefore, I believe that Schizophrenia would have been the most likely diagnosis.[2]

Q) Was it difficult to write a character with a mental illness? How did you approach this topic respectfully?

I don't think it was difficult to write Selena's character, but I also didn't think of her as a character with mental illness, either. I thought of her as a woman who has been dismissed and gaslit for her entire existence. She knew the truth of what happened to her, but because other's couldn't wrap their minds around her experience, they simply claimed it wasn't real.

As far as representing characters with mental illnesses, I think it's important to do your research and try to represent that disability as truthfully as you can. I myself struggle with mental illnesses, and I know how these things can hinder one's life and be perceived negatively by others.

In the end, I tried to think about my characters as people and treat them/represent them in the way that I would want my friends and family to be represented. The focus here was less on the perceived mental illness than on the way others tend to treat people with mental illnesses, allowing me to construct social commentary and hopefully open a few eyes, too.

Q) In *Dealings in the Dark*, there was an emphasis on the magick present in Alex's family lineage. Does Selena possess any magickal qualities?

Unlike Alex, when not possessed by a demon, Selena and her family do not possess any magickal lineage. She was the wrong little girl who lived on the wrong street at the wrong time. Selena, being roughly the same age as Alex, was an easy pawn for the female demon to use in her little game.

Q) Why doesn't the female demon have a name?

Part of the reason the female demon doesn't have a name is that it's a tactic she uses to torture Selena. She refuses to separate her own identity from Selena's identity, therefore effectively claiming that Selena never was and never will be her own person.

I am also a firm believer that names have power. If the female demon were to reveal her name, that information could be used against her. For example, Elizabeth Hendricks, Alex's grandma in *Dealings in the Dark*, was able to research and learn a great deal about Iroth. She used this information to anticipate some of his behaviors and trick him. This female demon does not want a similar situation to happen to her.

Q) Are the demons in your books specifically related to Christianity or another religion?

The demons in my Cursed Souls series are not specifically linked to any one religion. Instead, I think of them as magickal entities, or creatures, that have been called many things by many different cultures. Demon is just the most widely used term in the region where I live.

Q) ARE the demons in your books only able to inhabit one specific human being, or do they choose to inhabit the same person repeatedly?

The demons are actually able to inhabit as many people as they like, so long as they are inhabiting only one person at a time. With that said, some people are more susceptible to possession than others. The very young are easy to trick and manipulate. The elderly and the ill are physically weaker, and therefore less able to resist. Also, those who have already been possessed would be easier to possess again. So, Iroth and "Selena" could have chosen anyone to possess, but they chose these two individuals again purposefully for the impact that it would make upon Alex.

Q) WILL there be more books in the Cursed Souls series? If so, how long do you expect the series to be?

For now, the plan is to try to add at least two more books to the Cursed Souls series. However, sometimes life happens. There may be one more book, or there may be ten! Only time will tell.

Q) WHAT's next for Selena and Alex?

I guess you'll have to read the next book to find out!

. . .

Do you have questions for the author? If so, reach out to me at smoran@obsidianinkwell.com and you might have them answered! Thank you for reading *Bound and Betrayed*! I hope you enjoyed this novel. Please feel free to leave an honest review on Amazon or Goodreads. I look forward to writing for you again soon!

Bound and Betrayed on Amazon.com

Bound and Betrayed on Goodreads.com

1. "Schizophrenia." *World Health Organization*, 10 Jan. 2022, https://www.who.int/news-room/fact-sheets/detail/schizophrenia.
2. "Schizophrenia." Mayo Clinic, Mayo Foundation for Medical Education and Research, 7 Jan. 2020, https://www.mayoclinic.org/diseases-conditions/schizophrenia/symptoms-causes/syc-20354443.

SCHIZOPHRENIA RESOURCES

The events contained in this novel are entirely fictional. Hearing things that aren't there, seeing terrifying things that you shouldn't be seeing, or experiencing other events discussed in this text should not be dismissed.

If you or someone you know are experiencing symptoms that could be related to Schizophrenia, it's important that you talk to your doctor about them as soon as possible.

In the meantime, the following resources provide helpful information about Schizophrenia. Please be sure to use only information provided from scholarly sources when researching this mental health condition.

1. Mayo Clinic (MayoClinic.org)
2. National Institute of Metal Health (nimh.nih.gov)
3. American Psychiatric Association (psychiatry.org)
4. National Alliance on Mental Illness (nami.org)
5. World Health Organization (who.int)

*I am not a medical professional and am not qualified to give any sort of medical advice. These resources are provided purely for informational purposes.

**The websites presented in the printed text are abbreviated versions of the clickable link to the pages included in the e-text. To access specific pages on Schizophrenia, please utilize the search feature on the included sites. 194

ACKNOWLEDGMENTS

I want to say thank you to all of my readers who read and enjoyed Cursed Souls #1, *Dealings in the Dark*. In particular, I'd like to thank Marisol for immediately wanting a prequel and a sequel when she finished reading it. The first novella was meant to be a stand-alone horror tale, but because of the wonderful feedback from my readers, I decided to write a second book and even continue the series further! I loved getting to explore human Selena's perspective in the week leading up to the events of Alex's story. It was very fun weaving together the two tales. I wouldn't have done it without you.

Thank you to Marissa for always being my number one hype-woman.

I also want to thank my husband for supplying me with tea and snacks. I was very sick when I started working on *Bound and Betrayed*, so I couldn't have done it without you, either. I love you!

Finally, I want to thank my dog, Sugar. She kept my feet warm during these long nights of writing without ever complaining. I love you, Boo!

BONUS CONTENT

Thank you for reading *Bound and Betrayed*, the second installment in the Cursed Souls series. As a bonus, please enjoy this excerpt from *Apothecary of Curiosities: Volume One,* an award-winning collection of cozy horror tales.

(Note: This title is unrelated to the Cursed Souls series.)

Apothecary of Curiosities

Vol. 1

SAMANTHA MORAN

"DEATH'S NELL"

The brass bell above the door chimed as a woman strode through the entry, bringing with her a surge of wintry air and a flurry of snow. Death watched her with disinterest while she shook off her beret and dusted the slurry from the shoulders of her black, fashionable cape.

The woman had been here many times before, but not once had her presence brought with it a sale. At best, she was a detached visitor browsing the wares. At worst, she was a hovering nuisance. Nothing more.

Death straightened a newly polished assortment of athames, paying her little mind.

The newcomer tapped the toes of her stilettos on the rug, then moved to the far wall where she perused the shop's selection of fresh herbs. With each step came a resounding click. Her hand trailed along the edges of the baskets as she flipped through the meticulously labeled bags, finding nothing to her taste.

"Can I help you, Nell?" Death asked as she dusted her prized collection, a series of finger-length glass ampules of varying colors perched on a wooden display behind the register.

Nell paused by the table of raw and polished gems, hand hovering over an obsidian point. She blinked at Death, surprised the shopkeeper knew her name. As far as Nell could recall, she had never volunteered the information during her previous visits.

"Just browsing, I think," Nell answered. She tucked her thick mass of brown curls behind her ear and raised her eyes to meet Death's. "I doubt you have what I need."

Dismissively, Nell moved to the next table and thumbed through a collection of anatomical prints, examining a detailed image of the human heart.

"I have a great many things," Death answered, unperturbed. As though to demonstrate, she plucked one of the vials from its stand, holding it up to the light. Between her short, black nails, it glistened. The amethyst liquid splashed rhythmically from side to side, and a swirling silver strand spun within.

Nell's eyes widened as she realized what Death was holding. She dropped her hands to her sides, sliding her palms along the length of her tailored pencil skirt, smoothing away imagined imperfections in the fabric. Slowly, almost hesitantly, she approached the counter. Her pointed red nails tapped against the varnished oak as she eyed the vial. The knotwork ring on her finger glinted.

"So, it's true," Nell whispered. "You've bottled them."

Death cocked her head to the side, finally intrigued. She ran her free hand through the long, black strands of her shoulder-length hair. A glint of amusement sparked behind her dark eyes. "Them?"

"The sins. All seven of them. Is that what these are?" Nell gestured at the stand. "Your personal collection?"

Death flashed her a mischievous grin. "That depends. What interest would *you* have in sins?"

"May I?" Dodging the question, Nell confidently extended her hand.

Death considered the witch for a moment. The woman's avoidance hadn't gone unnoticed. Quite the opposite, in fact. Few refused to comply with Death's demands or willingly volunteer anything she wanted to know. Most were afraid of how she would react. But, there was no fear in Nell's expression, only fascination.

Perhaps she had been wrong about the woman. Not once had she spoken at length with the witch before. Their conversations had been only in passing. This was turning out to be an interesting day.

Death carefully placed the vessel into her customer's palm.

Nell reverently pinched the vial between her fingers and held it up to her eye. "Which one is this?"

"Why don't you tell me?" Death challenged. She leaned forward against the counter, propping herself up on her elbows. She lazily tipped her head into one of her hands and watched, amusement evident on her features. "Pop the cork. Give it a whiff."

Nell did as she was instructed. She twisted the cork from

the ampule's neck and set it on the counter, then brought the thin glass to her nose. She cleared her mind and closed her eyes, inhaling the heady scent: salt, strawberries, chocolate, and red wine.

"Mmm," she groaned, replacing the cork. "Lust. There's no doubt about that."

As she spoke, her mind filled with visions of the bottled sin. An unknown woman sank her fingers deep into Nell's hair. Sweat dripped down her spine, tracing a damp trail to her underwear. She felt a tug at the top as though someone desperately wanted them removed. Chocolate melted on her tongue, followed by a burst of sweetness, while the other woman licked at the corners of her mouth and nibbled at her lips. An electric hum shot through her core, leaving her trembling with desire. A throbbing began deep within.

"That was my first acquisition," Death replied. She lifted the ampule from Nell's hand, returning it to the rack. The swirling silver strand stilled, suspended in time. "Lust is easy enough to find. The soul contained here was young and reckless. She took many lovers to her bed before meeting her end at the hands of a rather jealous young man. Such a shame, but she does make a perfect addition to the collection, don't you think?"

Nell squirmed, crossing her legs. Gradually, the sensation faded, but the flush in her cheeks remained. "That was quite an experience. I can see why you chose her."

Death chuckled and plucked a second vial from the display. She passed it to Nell, who too eagerly accepted. The experience of inhaling the first sin had been nothing like she thought it would be. She couldn't wait to try it again.

"Identify them all, and there may be a surprise in store for you. I've been waiting for someone with a discerning mind such as yourself to take on the task. What do you say?"

"Why not? I have nothing but time," Nell replied. "I'm certain I can."

This new ampule contained a roiling ruby fluid. The swirling essence inside was golden, and unlike the last, it rocketed against the glass with impacts so forceful they shook the container in her grasp.

"Thoughts on this one?" Death asked as Nell struggled to hold the captured sin still long enough to remove the cork. "It's one of my favorites."

Nell finally tugged the cork free, then lifted the priceless extract to her nose. She cringed when the odor of pungent cigarette smoke, cheap whiskey, and iron overcame her. The sensation that washed over her as she passed the essence back to Death was far less pleasant than the first. Her head pounded, and her pulse thrummed in her ears. Nell balled her hands into tight fists, fighting back the sudden and over-whelming urge to strike Death, which common sense warned her would not be ideal.

Visions of broken bar stools and shattered glass populated her thoughts. She licked her bottom lip, drawing her tongue over an imaginary split in the skin and tasting the hot iron of blood. Her knuckles throbbed from insubstantial impacts. Her nails bit into her flesh, and every one of her muscles tensed. Massive invisible hands wrapped themselves around her neck, leaving her blood to pool in her face and making it difficult to breathe.

Through gritted teeth, she grunted, "That... has to be... wrath."

"Very good," Death offered, exchanging the vial for the next in line. "You have a knack for this. No one has been able to identify more than three. Would you like to try your hand with the next?"

The strangling grip on her neck released. Eager to forget

the sensation that had overtaken her, Nell nodded. "Yes, please."

"So polite," Death teased, dropping an emerald green bottle with a languidly glittering white cloud into Nell's outstretched hand.

There was no hesitation this time. Nell ripped the cork free and discarded it onto the counter, nearly spilling the liquid as she sniffed the contents. Anything had to be better than wrath.

There was an allure to the sin in this vial, but it lasted mere seconds before transforming into a horrendous stench. Immediately, she regretted her decision. Her stomach turned as she recognized rotten fruit and sour milk, followed by the bitter tang of cocoa nibs. Her body recoiled, drawing into itself. The lingering flavor of stale coffee settled onto her tongue. A sensation of absolute inadequacy washed over Nell. She swallowed down a mouthful of bile.

"Both wrath and this one were fairly simple to secure. I bottled the former at a bar down the way. He met an unfortunate end at the hands of his lover's father. Her daddy didn't take too kindly to the bruises on her face and neck. I'm sure that won't come as a surprise. And this one — "

"Envy... It's strong." Nell crossed her arms over herself protectively. The weight of soul-crushing depression pressed against her chest.

"So it was. As it often does, this particular sin manifested amongst siblings. Twins, in fact. Always competing. Always wanting to outshine the other, to have their own identity. In any competition, there must be a loser. Well, this twin has a special place of her own here on my shelf. What an honor. She was chosen. She won."

"I'm not entirely sure she'd feel the same way."

"Don't you know? The preferences of mortals mean nothing to me. I'll take them all in the end." Death played with the sharp pendant hanging from the chain around her neck, a dangling scythe. Her eyes flashed to the door and the city beyond. "She may as well serve a purpose."

"What purpose is that?" Nell spat.

"My amusement." Death replaced the cork and returned the tiny bottle to its place, pulling yet another from the display. "Eternity is a long time. I learned early on to seek my own entertainment, else the years grow increasingly dull. Unfortunate things occur when I'm bored, little witch."

Death tucked another vial into Nell's palm. The witch eyed Death with a mixture of respect and disdain. Still, no fear plagued her. That suited Death fine.

"Now, this one was harder to locate. See what you make of it."

Wary of the contents after the last two scents, Nell lifted the container and tried. At first, she smelled nothing. Death studied her expectantly as she sniffed the fluid, an absolutely still gray sludge, again.

A powerful punch of chemicals masked beneath a sweet scent burned her nostrils and brought with it an unfamiliar taste. Heaviness overtook Nell. Her arms slackened and the bones in her legs turned to jelly. They gave way, dropping her to the cold floor. The impact stole her breath. She struggled to right herself, but no matter how much she resisted, sleep threatened to claim her.

Warm molasses, maple syrup, and honey danced on the tip of her tongue. Heavy blankets and fluffy pillows pressed against her skin. Her eyelids slid closed and refused to open. She yawned, letting herself sink deeply into the experience of the sin.

"Now, that's an interesting reaction," Death mused. She craned her neck to see the slumbering woman curled up on the floor and folded her hands beneath her chin. "Wake up, little witchling."

When Nell didn't stir, Death rolled her eyes and stepped from behind the counter. She nudged the witch with the steel toe of her knee-high black boot, letting the metal spikes dig into her back. The witch jumped, waking with a start.

"Ow! What was that for?" Nell complained.

"I thought you were more capable than this." Death's words held disappointment as she lifted the vial and returned it to its place.

"More capable?" Nell felt the weight of exhaustion slip away. She pressed her palms against the marble tile and lifted herself to stand. Annoyance crept into her features. "You practically drugged me!" she accused. "What did you expect?"

"Resilience. You resisted lust, wrath, and envy. Who knew this one would do you in? What was it?"

"Sloth," Nell hissed, infuriated by Death's taunts.

"Correct. Perhaps this is too much for you. You should call it a day. Return to your shopping while I tend to the remaining sins."

Insulted, Nell huffed. "I've done better than anyone who came before me. You would send me away?"

"I would save you from yourself," Death calmly replied. Her black-tipped fingers danced across the fifth ampule of sin. "Or, I would offer you a chance to do so. Your choices mean little to me."

"You must think I'm weak," the witch challenged. "I'm not. Do you know who I am?"

"Very well," Death relented, handing her another container. "Your fate is in your hands."

Nell cracked the seal and held the shimmering bronze liquid up, inhaling deeply. The coppery tang of pennies, the musty scent of worn cash, and the sulfurous residue of gunpowder slammed into her like a hammer, knocking her several steps back. The vial slipped from between her fingers. She expected it to clatter to the floor, spilling its contents, but Death was there in an instant. The reaper snatched it out of the air and topped it with the cork, not bothering to help her customer, who clutched at her chest.

Fire ripped through Nell's lungs. Her heart beat so fast she could barely breathe. Her ribs wanted to bow to the will of the unseen projectile burying itself in her spine. Still, there was a craving. It tore at her core. *More... more... more... more!* Something fluttered in the air around her, brushing against her cheeks and hands. A metallic ting echoed through the shop, like coins falling to the ground.

"Greed," she eeked out through her gasps. "Money. What happened to this soul? It hurts..." Nell's muscles spasmed.

"Greed, indeed," Death crooned. "I warned you to turn back, did I not?"

"Yes, but — "

"It's never wise to ignore Death's warnings."

"I understand — "

"Yet, here we are. Can you feel his blood seeping between your palm and your chest? What's it like?"

The burning subsided, giving way to an incredible cold. Before Nell could open her mouth to speak, it was gone. She collapsed onto the counter, holding herself up by sheer force of will.

"I don't have the words."

"The man whose death you experienced was killed during a routine break-in. He and his friend chose the wrong house on the wrong night. The homeowner was armed and prepared. One 12-gauge blast to the chest stopped his greed dead in its tracks," Death chuckled. "Pun intended."

Death rolled the sixth bottle along the counter. The white

and clear fluid inside reminded Nell of separated milk. A foam crusted the top as Death removed the lid.

Nell, weakened by her brush with a shotgun moments before, lifted her trembling hand one more time. A heavenly aroma greeted her, and unconsciously, she licked her lips. It smelled of sugar, and cinnamon, and vanilla. Her stomach growled, longing for the pastries in the bakery window down the street.

The witch's mouth salivated, and a gnawing emptiness tugged at the depths of her stomach and intestines. She was starving. She felt as though she had never eaten before in her life. Not one bite of delicious food had ever passed her lips. All other thoughts fled her mind.

Death inspected the vial as Nell passed it back. She lifted the sin to her face and inhaled, too. The effect must have been diminished for the reaper because she didn't suddenly grow wild with need, but rather twisted her lips into a sympathetic smile.

Nell, on the other hand, doubled over. The ache of need in her abdomen radiated pain out to her limbs. She shook, and her teeth rattled. She bit her tongue and winced.

She could eat that, bite it off and swallow it whole. But, that was absurd. Why would she do that to herself? It was a demented thought brought about by the unbearable torment.

Death stoppered the bottle and returned it to the shelf. She plucked the final vessel from its place and set it on the counter before her.

Nell closed her eyes, willing the dregs of starvation away.

"Gluttony," she breathed. "I've never felt hunger so raw."

"And you never will again. That particular hunger came from an innocent babe, tossed to the street by its mother. It never knew sustenance, only pain. It would have consumed anything given the chance, and so I claimed it."

"An infant?" Nell balked. Her eyes grew wide. "But, they're innocent. No one should have to suffer like that. No one, especially not a child. Keeping it in that vial is cruel. It's vicious. It's *unimaginable*."

"It's a mercy," Death told Nell, her voice flat and bony fingers tapping on the oak. "Souls such as that one are devoured by the insatiable in the afterlife. This one survives, in a manner of speaking."

Tears sprang free from Nell's eyes.

"I've completed your challenge," she snapped. "All seven sins, identified."

Death nonchalantly shook her head. "Count again, witch. Six sins. Six vials. You have one more."

Nell's brow pinched in frustration. "The only one remaining is pride. I win."

"Do you?" Death raised an eyebrow. "That has yet to be seen."

With a huff, Nell straightened her clothes and stood tall. "What are you saying?"

Death didn't speak for a moment. Instead, she stared down at the bottle on the counter. The clear liquid shined. Slowly, she raised her eyes to meet Nell's. The look she gave the witch was forlorn.

"You haven't opened the last vial."

"Why should I? I know what it holds. By process of elimination. It's the only answer."

"You could walk away," Death offered. Her fingers splayed out on the countertop as she leaned forward. Death's lips brushed against Nell's ear, sending a chill down her spine. "No one requires you to play this game, little witchling. Turn around and leave my shop. Go back to your life. Have friends and family. Tell no one what you've experienced here. That's the safe option. *Choose life*."

"But," Nell began as she pulled away, "you won't admit that I won? That I completed the challenge?" Anger painted her words a vivid red. "That's ridiculous. I did as you asked. I defeated you at your own game. You're nothing but a sore loser."

Death threw up her hands as Nell snatched the last bottle. "By all means," she instructed, "open the ampule of pride."

A victorious smirk consumed Nell's features as she twisted the cork off the final bottle of sin. It fell to the counter with a series of muted thumps. Death watched her with a greedy stare as she raised the vial.

The container had no smell. No memories or visions flashed through Nell's mind. She blinked several times, willing the experience to begin, but it never came. Confused, she set the bottle aside.

"There's nothing," she said as she looked down at the empty glass. "Water? I don't know."

"The vessel is empty," answered Death with a sickening smile.

"But, why?"

Death rounded the counter, once more playing with the sharp-edged scythe dangling from the chain around her neck. She brought her hands to the back of her head and undid the clasp. The small charm slipped from the series of thin links and fell into the palm of Death's hands.

Nell took three steps back, bumping into the display of gems. They cascaded to the floor. Several shattered into jagged shards, and the witch slipped, landing hard on her back. The rough edges of the debris sliced into her forearms as she shoved herself away. Trails of bright crimson streaked across the floor, marking the witch's path.

Still, Death continued her advance. Her boots crunched over the remnants beneath her feet. The reaper's face split into a terrifying grin. Her eyes sunk deep into their sockets and her teeth sharpened. The illusion of clothes and human skin faded away, leaving nothing but gruesome skeletal remains.

Horrified, Nell watched as Death extended her arm and closed her bony hand around the charm. In a flash of fire and smoke, the talisman expanded into a functional weapon of solid wood and honed steel. Ornate designs decorated the shining blade. The reaper's fingers gripped the scythe so tightly, the handle groaned.

Whimpering, Nell continued to crawl away. She rolled from her back onto her stomach, rising to her knees and skittering across the floor. Death stalked her through the shop, never increasing her pace.

"Do you know why pride was the last of the sins?" Death questioned. Her voice was eerily steady and calm. "Why you couldn't turn away, no matter how many warnings I gave?"

The lights in the shop flickered, casting shadows across the reaper's face.

"No, no, no…" Nell begged as she reached for the heavy door. A blood-curdling scream broke free from her throat as she grabbed at the handle, finding it firmly locked in place. The brass bell jangled as she smacked her open palm against the glass. None of the pedestrians passing by spared her a glance. They couldn't see her, couldn't hear her.

"I told you to choose life," Death continued.

The reaper's footsteps grew closer, but Nell refused to look back. Instead, she pulled herself to her feet and searched for something, anything, she could use to break the pane.

"I told you to leave my store and go back to your family and friends, but you couldn't listen. You had to win. Had to play the game. Had to claim victory over the one thing all mortals, humans and witches alike, succumb to. Didn't you? I'd call you a fool," Death chided, kicking the obsidian tower away, "but that isn't it. It was pride, Nell. The final sin. The hardest to recognize."

Nell sobbed as she realized there was nothing within her reach. She was alone. She had been so stupid. Death was right. She should have walked away from the game, but she wanted to win. Why had she wanted to win? It seemed so pointless. A waste. A colossal mistake.

Turning around, Nell sniffed and wiped the snot and tears from her wet face. Streaks of blood smeared the places her hands touched. She dropped them to her side. "What now?" she asked, already knowing the answer.

Light sparked off the shining metal of the scythe as Death lifted it higher. "You wanted to see the game through to the end. This is how it goes. Your soul joins my collection. Sin number seven. The final piece of the puzzle. How prestigious."

"You didn't kill the others," the witch tried.

"I didn't have to. Their sins killed them for me. Except for the babe. The mother chose its demise."

Nell's eyes snagged on a sliver of hope and she stepped to the side. "My blood will be on your hands."

"Literally, I'd say so. But, the choice was yours entirely."

So, it was. Yet, she wasn't going down without a fight.

Nell slipped beneath Death's scythe and dashed for the obsidian tower, clutching it firmly in her grasp. She swung out with all her strength, sending the heavy stone crashing into Death's skull with a resounding crack. Death wobbled on her feet, but she didn't drop the weapon as Nell had hoped. The witch struck out again and again, each time connecting with a new bone.

The force of the impacts should have ground them into dust, but after the seventh blow, Death remained unchanged. The woman's arm, numb and weak, would not obey again. The stone tower fell to the ground as the witch collapsed, breathing raggedly.

Death bent down, bringing her empty eye sockets in line with Nell's. The reaper smelled of smoke and damp night air as she let out a sigh.

"I told you, little witchling. You should have chosen life."

Nell sobbed as the blade swung down. She shut her eyes, never to open them again.

Death wiped the crusted blood off the edge of the curved blade. The strip of fabric she had shorn from the witch's shirt did wonders for cleaning the engravings that ran down each side. As she worked, the enormous bell nestled in the steeple of the church at the end of the block chimed seven times. She allowed the scythe to minimize once more and slipped it back onto the chain, draping it around her neck and fastening it tightly.

Behind her, the securely stoppered seventh bottle churned, a shadowy mass of black with a core of gold. The pride of Death's collection.

From inside the ampule, Death could hear the soft sounds of Nell's eternal cries.

"They never learn," she declared as she once more dawned her human visage.

Death twisted the lock on the shop's door and stepped out into the night.

ABOUT THE AUTHOR

Photo Credit: Heavan Sent Photography

Samantha Moran (she/her) is an award-winning multi-genre author primarily focused on supernatural horror, thriller, and fantasy. She is fascinated by all manner of things that go bump in the night and strives to create relatable characters who face realistic problems in fictional settings. As her motto claims, she is a firm believer in the idea that "happily ever after is over-rated" and prefers her stories to be full of twists and mysteries.

Samantha holds a Bachelor's in English Secondary Education and is a proud Magna Cum Laude graduate of Western

Michigan University. (Go Broncos!) She is also a loving mother of two amazing children and has been happily married to her husband since 2015. She and her family reside in southwest Michigan, though she has also previously resided in the Baltimore, Maryland area.

Samantha lives with Multiple Sclerosis which sometimes severely impacts her daily life, especially her ability to use her hands.

In her free time, she loves tarot, playing *Dungeons and Dragons*, reading books, writing, and spending time with her family and dog.

For more information about Samantha Moran, or to keep up with personally published works, visit her website at www.samanthamoran.net.

BOOKS BY SAMANTHA MORAN

Cursed Souls:

Dealings in the Dark

Bound and Betrayed

Legacy of Lies (Coming Soon)

Standalone Works:

Without You

The Ruin

For the Dark and Depraved:

Wicked Little Rabbit

"As Brittle As Bone" (Coming Soon)

The Apothecary of Curiosities Short Stories:

Apothecary of Curiosities: Volume One